HANGING
BY A
THREAD

HANGING
BY A
THREAD

SOPHIE LITTLEFIELD

DELACORTE PRESS

Text copyright © 2012 by Sophie Littlefield
Jacket art copyright © 2012 by Weronika Mamot

All rights reserved. Published in the United States by Delacorte Press, an imprint of Random House Children's Books, a division of Random House, Inc., New York.

Delacorte Press is a registered trademark and the colophon is a trademark of Random House, Inc.

Visit us on the Web! randomhouse.com/teens

Educators and librarians, for a variety of teaching tools, visit us at RHTeachersLibrarians.com

Library of Congress Cataloging-in-Publication Data
Littlefield, Sophie.
Hanging by a thread / Sophie Littlefield. — 1st ed.
p. cm.
Summary: When a third person in three years goes missing, presumed dead, July Fourth weekend in Winston, California, sixteen-year-old budding fashion designer Clare Knight uses her gift of seeing visions of people's pasts while touching their clothing to seek the truth, at risk of her own life.
ISBN 978-0-385-74104-0 (hc) — ISBN 978-0-375-98982-7 (lib. bdg.) — ISBN 978-0-375-98356-6 (ebook)
[1. Mystery and detective stories. 2. Fashion design—Fiction. 3. Psychic ability—Fiction. 4. Missing persons—Fiction. 5. Single-parent families—Fiction. 6. Family life—California—Fiction. 7. California—Fiction.] I. Title.
PZ7.L7359Han 2012
[Fic]—dc23 2011047773

The text of this book is set in 12-point Adobe Caslon.

Book design by Stephanie Moss

Printed in the United States of America

10 9 8 7 6 5 4 3 2 1

First Edition

For Barbara Poelle

I couldn't do it without you—and even if I could,
it wouldn't be any fun.

Acknowledgments

With many thanks to my editor, Krista Vitola, for turning a lump of ideas into a story and then polishing it to a shine. Thank you, dear family, for carrying on splendidly through one crisis after another so that I could finish my work. My friends: you're everything to me, never more than this past year.

And thank you to Maddee James, Web maven and so much more—I can never appreciate you enough.

HANGING
BY A
THREAD

CHAPTER ONE

THEY SAY OUR HOUSE IS CURSED, and maybe it's true. It's been in my mom's family for almost a hundred years. It was a dress and alterations shop until ten years ago, when my mom and dad poured all their money into restorations so we could live in it. As soon as it was finished, they got divorced and we all moved away. But that's getting ahead of the story.

Three weeks ago, my mom and I moved back to town. We were finally getting around to hanging pictures on the walls, and the first one we pulled out of the moving box was of my great-great-grandmother Alma. In the old black-and-white photograph from the 1920s, she's standing in front of this same house.

The image is of Alma in her early twenties and very pregnant. She looks pretty in her simple wool serge dress. But she's overshadowed by the young woman standing next to her, who is wearing a gorgeous wedding gown. Silk voile drapes the bodice and dropped waist, and the Cluny lace veil is accented with small white feather plumes and pearls. If you look carefully, you can detect a darkness, a hint of fear, behind the young woman's shy smile.

The day after the picture was taken, both Alma and the young bride were dead.

. . .

I hung the picture while Mom watched, hands on her hips, directing me to move it a little higher, a little to the left. She's a perfectionist. I'm the creative type. Needless to say, this caused problems in our relationship, but we were treating each other gingerly. The move had caused enough stress already, and we were one sharp word away from a meltdown.

I wasn't exactly thrilled about leaving my old high school in the city and coming back to a tiny town where I only had one friend, but I was determined to make the best of it. I'd lived in Winston until I was ten, and I'd kept in touch with my best friend, Rachel, ever since. She'd grown up to be beautiful, popular, and—thanks to her dad's involvement in several start-up companies that had done well—rich, and she'd promised to get me connected with the in crowd at Winston High.

This was my big chance to finally fit in. Don't get me wrong—I'd loved my two years at my private arts high school. It was where I got interested in fashion design, and I'd made some good friends. But I'd had enough of the artistic temperaments competing for attention at the Blake

School, enough of the drama and the edginess of the San Francisco art scene. I was tired of sharing a cramped two-bedroom apartment with my mom. I just wanted to know what *normal* felt like, and a sleepy little beach town with a population of two thousand people seemed like the perfect place to find out.

My mom wasn't adapting very well to being back, however. When we'd moved three hours north six years earlier, it was like she decided to put her entire past behind her, not just my dad. She broke contact with all her old friends and threw herself into her new job in the city. As the years passed, she changed. She became more polished, more professional, and more distant.

When my dad lost his job a few months ago and couldn't keep up with his child support payments, private school was suddenly no longer an option. Then rents went up in our building, and the accounting firm my mom worked for was hit hard by the economy and she lost some important clients. When my dad offered to sign over his share of the house in Winston, she saw a solution to our problems. She bought out a small accounting firm in town from a man who was retiring, the renters moved out of the old dress shop, and we moved back as soon as school was over.

"So sad," she sighed, once I'd hung the photograph exactly where she wanted it, in the small foyer of our house. "Poor Alma."

It's the exact same thing she said when I hung the photo in the San Francisco apartment. I remember because I didn't know the story back then and I wanted to know what was so sad about it. My mom gave me a watered-down version, but later I got the whole story from my grandmother.

Back in 1923, Alma was a newlywed herself, excited about the arrival of her first child, planning to quit her job at the dress shop after giving birth. Her last big project was a wedding dress for a beautiful young woman engaged to a violent and jealous man named Forrest Hansen. Hansen had accused his fiancée of secretly seeing another man, an attorney in town, and though she'd denied it, she made the mistake of stopping to talk to the attorney one day when they met in the street. Hansen followed her to the shop that evening, waiting in the shadows outside while Alma made a few final alterations and a photographer took the bridal portrait for the newspaper. After the photographer left, Hansen stormed into the shop, yelling accusations. While the lovers argued, Alma must have tried to intervene, because after shooting his fiancée, Hansen shot Alma too.

She lived long enough for her baby to be taken from her that night. The coroner wrapped the baby in the wedding dress, which was lying nearby on the cutting table, to keep her warm. The baby was a healthy girl—my great-grandmother Josie—who would go on to work in this same dress shop when she grew up.

Hansen was caught, tried, and executed. But something else happened that night. Amid the terrible storm of jealousy and rage and violence, Alma's innocent baby was born with a strange gift, one that she passed along to one of her own daughters—my Nana—and eventually, when I was twelve years old, to me.

"Well, I've got to get over to the office," my mother said, yawning. There was a lot of paperwork she still had to do in order to transition the prior owner's clients.

"Rachel and I are going downtown to sell," I reminded her. Rachel and I had started a business together, selling my one-of-a-kind fashions. We'd done pretty well last weekend, and I was hoping we'd sell even more today.

"Okay. Good luck. I left you some money on the counter if you want to get lunch in town."

"We're going to the beach tonight." I said it in a rush, hoping Mom would let it go for once. Rachel's friends' standard Saturday night outing was to meet down at Black Rock Beach, build a fire, play volleyball until it was dark, and then sit and talk until midnight. For the last two weeks, she'd invited me along. I lived close enough to walk home— our town was small enough that you could walk from one end to the other in half an hour—but Mom still wasn't happy about it.

"Oh, Clare . . . ," she said, dismayed. "Can't you guys just go to someone's house? Or get a pizza or something?"

"Come on, Mom, it's only June twenty-ninth. Four more days until the madman strikes again."

"That's terrible—don't joke about it!" Mom exclaimed. She was more upset than I'd realized.

"Haven't you seen all the extra security they're bringing in for the festival?"

"Not at the beach."

"Well, they don't want kids hanging around in town while they're setting up. Where are we supposed to go?"

"You could always invite your friends here."

I rolled my eyes. Yeah, right, like Rachel's friends would want to come to my house. I was hoping to keep a low profile, and not just because I was the new girl. Our family had kind of a reputation in town. When I was little everyone used to say the old dress shop was haunted by my great-great-grandmother and the young bride who had been killed there. They said the reason my parents got divorced was that the house had cursed them. And when people in Winston got tired of gossiping about the rest of my family, my eccentric grandmother gave them plenty to talk about. I was learning that that was the downside of small-town living—everyone knowing everyone else's business.

"Nothing's going to happen," I said, with feeling. "Whoever did it, he's long gone. Besides, this town's going to be crawling with tourists and cops. It'll be like the safest place in the state."

I held my breath, hoping I hadn't pushed too far—tourism was still way down since the murders these last two Fourth of July weekends—and after a moment, my mom nodded. "Okay. But make sure you have a buddy when you're going up and down the path, and don't go in the water after dark, and—"

"Mom."

She stopped midsentence and gave me a crooked frown, hugging herself. For a moment she looked worried and fearful, nothing like the polished professional I was used to seeing walk out the door in the morning, dressed in her boring power suits, with her heavy bag over her shoulder.

"I'll be careful, okay? Promise."

Mom hesitated for a moment. I knew she wanted to say something else, but we'd made a habit of not saying some of the most important things. And when she hugged me, her familiar perfume seemed tinged with the scent of regret.

CHAPTER TWO

IT TOOK ME LONGER THAN USUAL to get dressed, which is saying something, since I always put a lot of time into choosing what I wear. Not just because I make a lot of my clothes myself, but because someday my look will be my brand. Kind of like Betsey Johnson—if you look at pictures of her from the eighties, you can see the inspiration for everything she's designed ever since.

But I'd be downtown, where everyone in Winston could walk by and see me. Did I really want to give them more reason to think our family was different? Maybe I could ease slowly back into my own style after starting out like everyone else. I went through my closet, picking out my most conservative clothes, which were basics I hadn't gotten around to altering yet: plain black canvas shorts, a gray tank top I layered under other clothes. I dressed and stared at myself in the mirror, hating the way I looked.

I knew my mom had struggled when she was my age.

She didn't talk about it much, but I got the impression that Nana had embarrassed her, and she'd spent her teenage years trying to simply disappear. It was different for me. I wanted to fit in but not blend in.

Stripping off the boring clothes, I tried again. I picked a fringed black ultrasuede miniskirt to go with a halter top I'd sewn from blue gauzy fabric that I'd gathered and twisted and then stitched into place. I borrowed my mom's cameo necklace and added a clip I'd made out of a long blue feather and a few strands of fake electric blue hair.

Way better. Now I felt like myself again.

The doorbell rang, and as I went to answer it, I checked myself out in the hall mirror and was satisfied with what I saw. Maybe my look wasn't for everyone, but it represented what I did best, and it would promote my business. Besides, a few of Rachel's friends had already asked me if I could make them one-of-a-kind pieces, so I knew there was a market for what I had to offer. Nana had been telling me for years that if I did what I loved, success would follow. It was yet another thing that drove my mom crazy—but then, she's an accountant, so her motto would probably be something more like "Do what pays the bills, and financial security will follow."

I opened the door to find Nana standing there. "I was just thinking about you!" I said, giving her a hug and pulling her inside with a guilty pang. I wanted to get her off the porch so people wouldn't see her—although the red VW bug covered with bumper stickers parked in front of our house was a dead giveaway.

Nana was impossible to miss. Her hair was a mass of silver ringlets that came down to her shoulders—unless she put it up to get it out of the way, in which case it burst out of the top of her head in all directions. She was a startling dresser, but unlike me, she didn't put a lot of thought into her outfits. I think she put on the first thing she grabbed in the morning, but since she had a fondness for bright colors and shiny fabrics and ethnic details and bought most of her wardrobe from the Indian import shop, the effect was usually blinding. And she'd been this way forever; in pictures from when my mom was little, Nana looks pretty much the same, except her hair used to be brown and her face less wrinkled.

She had a fondness for bright orange lipstick too, and I automatically wiped where she had kissed me, knowing from experience that she left marks. "Mom made coffee, I think. Want some?"

"Yes, better pour me a cup. She makes the best coffee anywhere—glad she hasn't given that up too." Nana loved my mom's cooking. When my parents split up, Nana told her she ought to become a chef or start a catering business—to do what she loved—which I could have told her would pretty much ensure Mom would never cook again.

We took our coffee out to the back patio. "I see your mom hasn't made much progress on the garden yet."

That was an understatement. The renters had left the tiny yard and flower beds alone; they were tidy but bare. "That's your thing, Nana. Mom's working so much I wouldn't be surprised if it stays like this for years."

"I could put in some bare-root roses this fall. You know what would be great along the fence? Some canna, maybe red ones—"

"Nana," I interrupted. "Mom would kill you."

She sighed. "I know, I know, and I'm trying to keep my distance and wait for an invitation. But you know, you're welcome to come on up the hill anytime, even without your mom."

I couldn't meet her eyes. I'd only visited twice since we moved back, and we both knew I'd been avoiding her. But I wasn't sure if Nana understood how much rode on this summer, on me making new friends before the start of my junior year. And there was no way for me to explain without her knowing the truth, which was that I didn't want to be associated with her, at least not in public. Not until I had gotten established here.

"Are you going to the festival?" I said, changing the subject.

"Yup, I'm going to be at the loggerheads booth in the morning and then we're protesting at the dedication of the new gazebo in the afternoon."

"Oh, Nana . . ." My heart sank. Nana and her weird friends had made the papers before, half a dozen old hippie types carrying signs and marching around downtown. "What is it this time?"

"Have you seen the corporate sponsor list?" she demanded, outraged. "Taking money from big oil? Defiling our most precious resources just so we can spruce up the town for a bunch of tourists?"

"Okay, okay, I get it," I said, making a note to be elsewhere during the ceremony.

"But that's not why I came over," Nana said, her expression softening. "Listen, honey, I know you've heard it a million times, but you have got to be careful this week. Lock the doors at night, stay in a group, call me or your mom if you need a ride."

"Oh, Nana, not you too."

"It's not just me. Everyone in town is worried about you kids."

"Nana, that's all hype. The media just wants to stir things up for ratings."

On July third the last two years in a row, terrible things had happened in Winston. Two years ago, a ten-year-old boy named Dillon Granger had been killed. It was made to look like an accident—his body had been found next to his mangled bike on the rocks below a sheer cliff—but forensics revealed bruising and damage to the bike that suggested he'd been pushed. An anonymous 911 caller reporting an accident along the cliff road was considered a suspect, but the recording of the call, made from a local truck stop pay phone, was muffled and unclear. They couldn't determine anything about the caller's identity, not even age or gender.

And this past July third, a high school girl named Amanda Stavros disappeared without a trace. As time went by and no evidence of her was found, she was presumed dead.

Dillon's death was reported all over California. We watched it on the news up in San Francisco—the footage of the road above the sheer cliff, the grieving parents at the funeral service. Mom knew the mother slightly, but she'd still been in middle school when Mom went off to college.

When Amanda disappeared, we were glued to the TV night after night. After police let it slip that they thought the deaths could be connected, the story made national news. Grim-faced newscasters reported that the crimes were suspected to be the work of a serial killer, and predicted that it might happen again. There were interviews with detectives and criminal psychologists. Rewards were offered, federal agencies called in, tips followed up on, persons of interest interviewed, but no arrests were ever made.

Mom and I had watched it all. She had made a clean break from Winston, but she'd grown up here, as had I, and we couldn't take our eyes away from reports showing familiar scenes of town. Also, she'd gone to high school with Mrs. Stavros, though they hadn't been close friends. Mrs. Stavros had been popular and beautiful—she'd even modeled for a while after graduation, and her magazine photos ended up in the news, along with details of her husband's business dealings. Reporters camped out in front of their house, the coffee shop where they were known to go in the mornings, even the salon where Mrs. Stavros got her hair done.

As the months went by, the story kept coming back on the news whenever details emerged: The little boy was suspected of having been beaten before his body was tossed into the sea. Amanda's boyfriend had been questioned by the police. Her father had hired independent detectives. Rewards were doubled, then doubled again.

As we were getting settled in after the move, *Newsweek* ran an article with the headline "One Year Later: Town Braces for the Worst," making it sound like the killer was expected to show up for the third year in a row. But the Winston Chamber of Commerce was fighting back. The Independence Day festival was taking place on July third, to draw attention away from the anniversary of the murders, and the town was pulling out all the stops to attract tourists. There would be entertainment, food, and a fireworks display to rival San Francisco's. And there were rumors that the town had hired tons of security, both plainclothes and uniformed.

"You can't be too careful," Nana said. "Besides, he's going after kids like you."

"Like *me*?"

"The stars. The best and brightest. The cream of the crop."

"Oh, Nana . . ." I knew what she was implying: Dillon had been a star baseball player, even at the age of ten. He'd been on a team that went to the Little League World Series the year before he was killed. And Amanda had been pretty and popular and a good student. She'd been captain of the JV cheer squad and a member of the Gold Key Society, an exclusive girls' service club at Winston High, which must have been a good human-interest angle because the newspapers ran stories about it. "No one knows me here, and besides, I'm hardly a *star*."

"Clare, you're wonderfully talented, and beautiful! Look at you!"

It was the sort of thing Nana always said, and there was no way I was going to convince her otherwise. "Okay. I'll be careful. I'll come straight home from the festival and lock myself in with Mom. We'll bar the doors and get out the shotguns. Happy?"

"You just make sure you do that. And call me. Promise?"

"Promise."

She finally seemed to relax. "Now show me what you made this week."

Nana was my number-one fan, and she was also the only other person in my life who knew anything about sewing, so I loved showing her my work. I made clothes and bags from other people's castoffs, taking them apart and sewing them back together again, tailoring sleeves and hems and necklines, and adding trim and embellishments.

This week I'd altered a coral-pink jacket that came from a suit my mom hadn't worn in years. I'd added bright orange piping around the lapels, and replaced the buttons with vintage stamped-metal ones from the sixties. As a final touch I'd sewn on a pink and coral fabric flower that came from one of my old headbands.

A pair of jeans—size 2, three sizes too small for me or I would have kept them for myself—now sparkled with bugle-bead curlicues starting on the back pockets and trailing down the outer seams of the legs.

And finally there was a tote bag stitched together from pieces of an old brown and pink quilt I'd salvaged. The quilt had been falling apart—someone had used it so many times that the binding had frayed and some of the patches had holes—but there were sections that were perfectly good. I carefully cut these out, sewing them to brown corduroy panels cut from a pair of men's Levi's. I'd added a heavy-duty zipper with chrome teeth and handles made from left-over corduroy. When I'd finished it the night before, I thought it had a funky charm, but now I wondered if it was just plain ugly.

"You've outdone yourself!" Nana laughed as I slipped my creations into my backpack.

I wasn't sure that was a good thing. Nana's style was the last thing I wanted mine to resemble. Still, she complimented everything I did—I could make a skirt out of a garbage bag and she'd tell me it was gorgeous—so I let it go.

"I have to run, Nana," I said. "I'm meeting Rachel at ten."

"Just remember what I said."

I promised her yet again, then waited until I heard her car puttering down the hill before I wheeled my bike out to the street.

Be careful. Stay in groups. Lock the door.

And don't end up being Winston's third Independence Day murder victim.

CHAPTER THREE

I RODE MY BIKE DOWN THE HILL to a restaurant called the Shuckster. Rachel couldn't pick me up in her Nissan 370Z because our sales booth took up her passenger seat. Its wooden legs jutted straight up, and whenever the canvas top caught the wind, she had to hold on to it with her free hand to keep it from flying out of the car and into traffic. It had taken a lot of work to convince Rachel's mom that Adrienne, Rachel's nine-year-old sister, had outgrown her puppet theater and wouldn't mind if we used it to sell my one-of-a-kind creations. And it had taken ten bucks to convince Adrienne, which put me in the hole for this venture before we even started.

When Rachel found out we were moving back to Winston, it had been her idea to start a business together. She'd seen the things I made the few times I had visited her, and thought we could make a lot of money selling them. Of course, she didn't need the money—but she did need a summer job, because her mother insisted she do something other than lie around the house all day.

The puppet theater "storefront" had been her idea, and she did the merchandising, too. The way she figured it, people were a lot more likely to stop and look at our wares if they were displayed at eye level. We hung my creations from nails we pounded into the theater's frame, and on the front we displayed the sign we had made on Rachel's computer and laminated at the copy shop. It had turned out great—the words "NewToYou" in bright pink curlicue font on a pale orange background. We'd thought about adding a second line of text beneath the name—"Everything old can be new again" or "New life from old duds," but neither one got across the message we wanted.

Which was *cool*. We wanted people to think restyled vintage clothes and accessories were cool. It didn't hurt that Rachel was a trendsetter at Winston High; if she put her seal of approval on something, everyone else liked it too. I'd been skeptical at first, but when some of her friends stopped by our stand last week and bought things, I had to admit that Rachel's idea had been brilliant.

"Hey hey, Cee-Cee girl!" Rachel yelled as she swerved in next to the curb, the stand bobbing dangerously in the passenger seat. I ran to steady it, grimacing at Rachel's nickname for me.

I really wanted to be known by the name I'd had since I was born sixteen years and three months ago. But Rachel's whims were as contagious as they were unpredictable. Already, half the kids I knew had started calling me Cee-Cee too, and since I'd met them all through Rachel, odds were they'd keep doing it as long as she did.

"You're only ten minutes late this time," I said as we got the stand out of the car. "That's some kind of record."

"Yeah, but that's because I had to take Adrienne to camp. Mom said if I was late again she was going to make me volunteer there. God, can you imagine—twenty fifth-grade girls doing *crafts*?"

She made a face, thoroughly disgusted by the idea, so I didn't bother to point out that what I did was just a more sophisticated version of the loopy potholders and dish-towel pillows the girls made. When I was their age, I loved those crafts; anything that involved a needle and thread had captivated me as far back as I could remember, ever since Nana started letting me play with her boxes of scraps and buttons and bits of ribbon and lace.

I hauled the stand out of the car, and the big plastic storage tub out of the trunk, and started setting it all up. First I hung all the things that hadn't sold last Saturday, using the curved safety pins I got at a quilt shop. They were thin enough not to damage any of the fabrics, and the shape made it easy to attach them to the canvas or hook over nails. I hung hats and bags along one side, tops and skirts along the other, the fabrics overlapping to make a crazy rainbow that flapped gently in the breeze.

Once all the older pieces were displayed, I dug into my backpack for the three new pieces I'd made this week, hanging these along the top crossbar of the stand.

Rachel was watching me, hands on hips.

"So, what do you think?" I said, stepping aside to give her an unobstructed view.

"We'll sell those jeans by ten-thirty," Rachel said without hesitation. "The jacket's going to take longer, but we'll get some lady from the suburbs down here for the weekend. But that bag? It's like someone was smoking crack at the quilting bee, Cee-Cee, are you *serious*?"

I touched the soft, worn patchwork of the bag. So maybe the plastic elephant head I'd used for a closure—I found it at a garage sale and drilled a hole in it so I could sew it on—was a little over the top.

But over the top was what I did. It was who I *was*.

"I'll bet you a Hoff run," I said, straightening the bag. "Someone's going to love this."

Rachel snorted. "Yeah?"

"Yeah."

"If you're so sure . . ." She dug into her purse for a Sharpie and wrote on one of the pink cardboard tags we'd made one night while watching *Princess Bride* for the millionth time. Rachel did the tags because she had prettier handwriting.

When she held it up she looked smug. She had written *$55,* and I shook my head as she carefully attached the tag to the bag's strap and then curled the tag's silvery ribbon with a pair of safety scissors.

"If I can get fifty-five bucks for it by noon, the Hoff run's on you."

"Just because I said someone is bound to love that bag doesn't mean you can price us out of the market," I complained.

"You said you were sure," Rachel reminded me. "Besides, someday you're going to be famous, and this'll be worth a fortune."

· · ·

The jeans sold first, just as Rachel predicted—a woman with giant sunglasses bought them for one of her two cranky daughters, bargaining us down from thirty to twenty-six dollars. But the crazy quilted bag wasn't far behind. At eleven-forty-five, after we'd been in business for less than two hours, an older lady with short white hair walked by the booth with a small brown fluffy dog on a leash—and did a double take.

"Monkey puzzle!" she exclaimed.

"Um . . . excuse me?" I had been reading an article titled "What He's Thinking When He Gets Dressed" in the June issue of *Glamour*. Mom brought old magazines home from the office whenever new issues arrived. Her accounting business was located in a bungalow that also housed a dental practice, and I guess none of the staff wanted the old magazines.

"This quilt block—its name is Monkey Puzzle. My grandmother made a quilt like this—well, not like this, exactly." The white-haired woman laughed, her raspy voice warm and friendly. "My grandmother probably never would have thought of using an elephant."

I blushed. Okay, so maybe the elephant head hadn't been my best idea ever.

"Uh, well, we have some really sweet little zipper cases that are also made from salvaged quilts," I mumbled, sorting through the rack. "Perfect for holding makeup, or eyeglasses—"

"Oh, no, honey, I like this one." She laughed again as she handed the bag to Rachel to wrap up. "You've got quite an eye. May I ask where you find your merchandise, girls?"

"Clare sews each piece herself," Rachel said proudly. She called me by my real name in front of adults, for which I was grateful. "Everything's made right here in Winston."

The lady raised a silver eyebrow. "Clare *Raley*?" she asked. "Lila's granddaughter?"

I smiled uncomfortably. "Clare Knight, ma'am, actually. But yes, Lila Raley is my grandmother."

"Oh, of course you wouldn't be a Raley, what was I thinking? Your mother married that boy she met in college."

"Joe Knight," I said, blushing harder as I got ready to tell my usual lie. "Although my mother and father are amicably separated."

"Yes. Yes. Well." She didn't stop smiling, even as her expression slipped just a bit. Rachel counted out change and handed it over. "I should have known your creativity runs in the family. Lila's quite a character, isn't she."

That was code for "eccentric." People had a lot of different ways of saying it, but I knew what they meant—my grandmother was weird. I sighed. "Yes, ma'am."

"And so *active* locally, with all her causes. Now if we could just get her to put some of her energy into restoring that lovely historic home of hers, hmm?" She gave me a smile to mask the fact that she'd just insulted Nana's house. Many Winston residents thought Nana had turned the old Raley mansion into an eyesore. "You be sure to give her my regards, all right? And your parents, too."

As I watched the woman walk away with her new tote bag tucked under her arm, I wondered what she would think if she knew that I hadn't seen my father, Joe Knight, in almost a year, despite the fact that he lived only three hours away. Or that Nana was planning to paint her front door purple.

Or that while I was cutting up the corduroy jeans that became the handle of her new bag, my mind had filled with visions of the man who'd worn them the night he'd robbed a convenience store.

CHAPTER FOUR

CLOTHES SPEAK TO ME.

Not all clothes. And not all the time. It's been happening since before I was old enough to understand what my visions meant. No, strike that—I *still* didn't always understand what I saw, even after Nana shared what she knew about the gift she had passed down to me. She believed that what happened long ago on the night when Alma died was the direct result of a terrible kind of justice. Or rather, *the physical manifestation of a lack of balance created when there is an injustice.*

Those were her words, and I can still hear her saying them all these years later. I was twelve when she told me. I'd just started seventh grade and had my first vision, a silver-sparkled, hazy episode, when I borrowed my friend Gayle's sweater and, slipping it over my school uniform in the coatroom, got so dizzy I had to sit down. In the blurry moments that followed, feeling like I was watching a grainy television in my mind, I discovered that Gayle had dropped her mother's favorite vase out of a second-story window after she was grounded.

That night, I tried to talk to my mom about what had happened, and she lost it. She started yelling, and then she apologized, making me promise to forget what had happened and to tell no one about it, ever. She said it was like a disease, but if I ignored it, it would go away.

So when we drove down to Winston for Thanksgiving a few weeks later, I waited until my mom was busy with her laptop in the den, and whispered my forbidden questions to Nana. She took me into the kitchen with a worried look and, after cutting me a slice of pumpkin bread, told me that she'd always known I was special. That was when I found out what really happened to Alma.

"The baby who was born the night Alma died was my mother, Josie," Nana said after telling me the story of Alma's murder.

"Did she have it? The . . . *gift?*" I wasn't sure what I thought of Nana's term for it yet, especially since Mom's reaction had convinced me it was something terrible.

"I'm almost certain she did, though my memories from that time aren't very reliable. She died when I was still in my teens. But Mama always seemed to know things about people in town. And why wouldn't she? People brought clothes to the shop all the time. She'd take up a hem or alter a neckline or a sleeve, and once in a while she'd learn something about the person who wore it. I remember there were some families she wouldn't sit close to in church . . . a few kids whose houses she wouldn't let us go over to."

"Didn't you wonder why?"

"Well, I had bigger things to worry about. People said that our family was cursed. They started up all that nonsense about the shop being haunted. Kids at school used to tease me and Mary and Agnes; they said they could see Alma's ghost following us around, that kind of thing. I thought Mama was just trying to spare our feelings. After all, she grew up an orphan—she was raised by one of her aunts—and she was determined to give us a loving childhood." She smiled sadly. "I still miss her sometimes. Lord, but it's been a lot of years."

"But what did she say when you started doing it? When you had your first vision?"

"Well, I didn't call it that, of course. What happened was, we had a neighbor boy who was nothing but trouble. We lived a couple of miles out of town back then, next to a sheep ranch. Out where Via Loma cuts through now. Anyway, someone was leaving the gate open and the rancher had lost half a dozen sheep. That boy left his jacket over at our house one day, and when I touched it, I saw he was the one who'd been doing it—out of plain old meanness. I got a look inside his head that . . . Well, it's no surprise he ended up being nothing but trouble. Moved away a few years later, and I can't say anyone missed him."

"Did you tell your mom what you saw?"

"I did, and I'll never forget what she told me. She acted like it was the most natural thing in the world to see things in clothes, but said it was my choice whether to do anything with what I saw. She made it very clear that if something like that happened again, it wasn't my job to fix other people's mistakes, or to get involved at all."

"So did you? Get involved?"

"Sometimes I did. I learned that the greater the wrong, the stronger the vision could be. If someone had hurt someone else—if I thought there was danger of it happening again—then I'd try to help make it right. And years later, when I tried to stop, I learned that it was possible . . . just very difficult."

"What do you mean? How do you quit?"

"If you never do anything about what you see, if you make sure that you never get involved, never alter your behavior because of a vision, they'll slowly fade away and you won't get them anymore. And that's just fine," she added, in a voice that seemed tinged with sadness.

"Is that what happened to you?" I knew without asking that Nana didn't have the visions anymore. She was a lot of things—an artist, a gardener, a cook, a planet-saver—but I'd never known her to get involved in other people's business.

"Yes," she said, and stared out the window, her eyes filled with regret.

"What?" I demanded. "What happened?"

"That's not a story for today," Nana said, suddenly sounding tired. "Actually, that's not a story for me to tell at all."

CHAPTER FIVE

Rachel waited until the woman who had bought the tote bag was out of earshot before holding her hands up above her head and making the victory sign.

"Hoff run," she said in a singsong voice. I grimaced, but there would be no getting out of it. I'd lost the bet, fair and square.

"Hoff run" was short for "Hasselhoff run," which in turn was our nickname for the cost of doing business here in front of the Shuckster. The casual seafood restaurant and bar hadn't been our first choice as a location to set up shop. It hadn't been our second, either, or our third, fourth, tenth, or twenty-second. No. The Shuckster was dead last on our list of the twenty-three merchants on either Beach Road or Shore Street, which made up the entire downtown business district of Winston, California.

The Chamber of Commerce website said that the local population of 2,100 swelled by thousands because of tourists every summer, but I was pretty sure they hadn't updated the site since the murders. I had checked the website to find out if it really was true that hawking merchandise without a license was punishable by jail time. We were told this once by the cranky, chain-smoking man who owned Seaside T's and Gifts when he told us to get lost. It wasn't— but there *was* a town ordinance and a fine of $250, a fact that was confirmed by the cop who stopped us as we came out of Earl's Old-Tyme Barber Shoppe after having been turned down yet again for our request to set up shop out front.

"But what you *could* do," the cop said as he stared at Rachel's bikini top, "is if you could find someone to sponsor you, and if you stayed on their property, well, I doubt we'd have a problem with that."

Sounded good to us, except that turned out to be an even harder sell to the merchants of picturesque Winston. With business down already, they didn't want to do anything that might put off potential customers.

Until we got to the Shuckster. As we'd climbed the steps to the broad wooden porch that day two weeks earlier, Rachel had put a hand on my arm to stop me. "Wait," she'd said, chewing her gum fiercely. Rachel might have looked like a Victoria's Secret model, but she could be surprisingly clever, so I waited patiently for her to think through whatever she was scheming.

"So here's the deal," she said after a moment. "The guy who used to own the Shuckster—Mr. Price? He's like a hundred. His son runs it now. He's a *major* creeper. I mean, he'll probably let us set up here, but he's a huge lech."

She shrugged. "I just want you to know what you're getting into."

I looked through the open door into the dim interior of the restaurant. I couldn't see much inside, other than a few neon beer signs and the bar itself, quiet now during the afternoon lull between the lunch and dinner rushes.

"So you're saying . . . I have to let him grab my ass if we want to set up here?"

"No, not at all. Just that you're going to have to stay on your toes. Oh, and Cee-Cee? He looks just like the Hoff."

"The who?"

"Hasselhoff. David Hasselhoff? You know, the disgusting guy from TV? He was on *Dancing with the Stars* a few years ago?"

And Mason Chase did resemble a young Hoff, with masses of messy brown hair and a leering grin and baggy, wrinkled surfer clothes. I figured he was about thirty years old, but you got the feeling he'd done enough partying for a lifetime. When he shook my hand, his eyes lingered on my body, and as he listened to our business proposal, he actually winked at me.

But Rachel assured me that we could handle him, and so, after exhausting every other possibility, we opened for business last Saturday and made almost three hundred dollars our first day, of which Rachel took sixty. She was content with twenty percent of the profits since, as she pointed out, I did all the design and sewing and her job was mostly to sit in her chair looking hot and talk to the customers. In fact, she offered to work for free because she didn't need the money, but I wasn't comfortable with that. I wanted to run NewToYou like the real business I hoped to own someday, when I would design my own line of clothing. If that meant sharing the profits with my employee and putting up with a difficult landlord, I'd do it.

. . .

And now it was my turn to pay up. Our "landlord" didn't charge us rent, but he said we should check in with him a few times every Saturday to let him know how it was going, which seemed to mean that he would pretend to talk business while he stared down our shirts and tried to accidentally brush against us as he offered us sodas.

I groaned, hauling myself up from one of the two folding chairs we dragged out of the Shuckster's storage shed.

"Wish me luck." I sighed theatrically.

"Luck," Rachel answered, already popping in her earbuds.

Inside, the restaurant was cool and smelled of stale beer. The floor was sticky, even though the late shift had supposedly washed it last night, and the Garza brothers were taking the chairs down, the sound system playing techno music.

What a life, I thought—setting up the bar each day, hauling in the ice, stocking the oysters and shrimp and crab, manning the hot grill, serving the sunburned tourists, listening to the same endless loop of music over and over again, finally going home smelling like beer and sweat, only to take a shower and come back to do it all over the next day.

But was it really so different from my mom's job? Every day she put on the same boring clothes and went to her tiny office and worked on her computer and dealt with her clients, none of whom she seemed to like very much, squinting through her reading glasses and adding up columns of numbers on her spreadsheets. At night, after we had dinner, she'd often take out her laptop and do more of what she did at the office.

The same thing, day in and day out. It was not the life I dreamed of. I wanted to design clothes, to work with models and manufacturers, to go to the shows and spot the trends—no, *set* the trends—and never, ever be bored. I wanted every day to feel like an adventure, and I'd work as hard as I had to, do whatever it took, to make sure that happened.

I told my mom I was saving for a car, and I was—but I had something else in mind too. I was determined to go to the Los Angeles Fashion Institute after high school. The problem was, my mom didn't think that was the same as college. She said a two-year associate's degree program wasn't a real education, and that she hadn't been building my college fund since I was two years old just to see me "waste it."

Okay, she'd only said that once—and she *did* apologize afterward. But I wasn't sure I could count on her support if I decided to go to the Fashion Institute over her objections. Besides, unless my dad started making good money again, he wouldn't be helping to pay for college either.

Inside the filthy little windowless room that Hoff used for an office, it smelled like an overdose of cologne with a hint of industrial cleaner, and I hesitated in the doorway.

"Cee-Cee," Hoff said, his eyes going straight to my body. It made my skin crawl, the way he looked me up and down, not even trying to hide it. "I was just going to mix up a couple of cold ones for you girls. Got this new one, we're calling it the Winston Wallbanger—vodka, orange juice, and a splash of Amaretto."

"I'm underage, Mason," I said for the tenth time. I was always worried I'd slip and call him Hoff. "I just wanted to say thanks for letting us set up again."

"How's business today?"

"Pretty good. Made a few sales."

"Hey, you know what you oughta do, you ought to start up a men's line, you see what I'm saying? Maybe do Hawaiian-type shirts, surf theme—"

"Thanks, Mason," I said quickly, "but I do all custom work. A lot of embellishment. Men aren't into that."

"Yeah, yeah, right," he said, as though we hadn't had this conversation before. He hauled himself out of the chair and came around his cluttered desk, so I started backing up.

He might have only been fifteen years older than us, but he hadn't seen the inside of a gym in a while, and he'd been helping himself from the bar and the grill on a regular basis. The net effect was that he moved like a guy twice his age.

That gave me an advantage, and I was halfway to the door by the time he caught up with me, handing over a couple of cold bottles of root beer. I closed my hand around the necks and dodged out of the way of his playful "hey buddy" slap on the back—the kind that if you didn't move fast enough turned into a sweaty hug—and was out the door, blinking from the sun.

Back at the stand, Rachel was talking to a boy I hadn't seen before, not someone from the crowd she usually ran with. He was at least a few inches taller than me, and I'm almost five nine, and had hair so dark it was nearly black, with glints of red-gold where the sun hit it. He was wearing a faded green T-shirt with a San Francisco State logo, and as I watched them talk, he crossed his arms and the sleeve slid up his bicep. I instantly learned two things: first, this boy worked out, and second, he looked great with or without the deep tan that ended where his sleeve did, the skin above his tan line golden and the skin below a burnished brown.

When I stepped in front of the stand, he pulled his sunglasses off and smiled. His eyes, big and brown with long lashes, were lit with a flicker of amusement, and for a moment I thought he was laughing at me. I hoped Rachel hadn't told him I was the person behind NewToYou and that he thought my stuff was ridiculous.

It wasn't just insecurity making me feel that way. I mean, it was, but I had my reasons. Not everyone loved my work, and even though I knew I had to get used to criticism, it was different here. At Blake, we were all into art. There were kids who did stranger things than fashion design—think sculptures made of lightbulbs and toilet paper, or digital "music" that included dolphin sounds and cowbells—so I felt relatively normal by comparison. But now that I was selling the things I made, I sometimes overheard things I wished I hadn't. One woman said "I wouldn't dress my dog in that," and a girl about my age told her friend it looked like we'd raided the Salvation Army, which was actually close to the truth, though I got my materials from all over the place—garage sales and thrift stores and friends and family.

I was working on not caring what people thought, but it was an uphill battle. I would never tell Rachel how glad I really was to have her around, because no one from Winston High would ever dare say anything negative when she was there.

"Cee-Cee, guess who came by—this is Jack Dimaunahan, remember? The one I was telling you about?"

"Um. Sure." Rachel had never mentioned anyone named Jack, but it was so like her to pretend we'd been talking about him just to flatter him. She couldn't *not* flirt; flirting was in her DNA. The trouble was, I had no idea what she had told him about me, if anything, and she wasn't above lying to make things more interesting.

"You went to Los Angeles Fashion Institute?"

Ah. Well, at least now I knew. I threw Rachel a glare, and then smiled sweetly at Jack. "Actually I only went to a summer program there, last year. For kids. You know, like camp? But I'm hoping to go there for real when I graduate next year."

Jack leaned his elbows on the wooden counter. He was close enough that I could smell him—salt and soap and a hint of sweat. But in a good way. I could see the faint shadow of his beard along his jaw, and he had a pale scar under his chin.

"I don't know much about fashion or design or whatever." He gave one of the small purses a shove, a square one made from a tweed jacket I'd found in a thrift shop in Oakland. I'd added red buttons in different shapes and sizes, sewn on in the shape of a heart. I'd been thinking someone might choose it for a little girl, but so far no one had shown much interest in it. "These are really . . . different."

He hated them, I was sure of it. My heart sank, even if he wasn't exactly my target audience.

"Jack plays soccer," Rachel said in a bored voice.

"What position?" I asked, then realized I didn't know if they even had positions in soccer. I'd been to exactly one game, when the Blake School lost to Ford Hills by a final humiliating score of five to zero. We were the zero, which you'd know without being told if you spent five minutes in the halls of my old school. We weren't exactly bursting with athletes, so it was quite a feat even to get enough kids together to make a team, and the only reason anyone went to the game was that the coach—who was also our art history professor—threatened to dock our grades if we didn't show up to cheer them on.

Jack shrugged indifferently. "Forward. But I'm not going to play this year."

"Why?" Rachel slipped the straps of her tank top down her shoulders—she was always concerned about tan lines. It was a move that usually got attention, but Jack kept his gaze on me, which gave me a shivery feeling. He wasn't smiling, but there was something in his expression, something more than idle curiosity.

"Well, for one thing, I'm not allowed back on the team since I got suspended. And besides, I need to work at my uncle Arthur's clinic."

"Huh. That's too bad." Rachel yawned, covering her mouth with her perfectly manicured fingers, clearly tired of the conversation. Probably because she wasn't the center of it.

"What kind of clinic?" I asked, wondering what he'd been suspended for, and figuring it must have been bad if he couldn't return to the team. But I didn't want Jack to leave. Rachel was signaling that we were done with him, as far as she was concerned. I glanced across the street and understood why: a green Land Rover LRX was pulling into a parking space—specifically, the green Land Rover that usually held Hopper Messerly, Rachel's current boyfriend, and Ky Muse, the boy she had a crush on. But they didn't see us and headed into the skateboard shop instead.

"Vet." For a second, Jack's scowl lifted. "North Shore Veterinary, out by the Beachview shopping center."

"I know it!" I exclaimed. The square brick building used to be an anonymous lawyer's office with no appeal at all. But when we came back to town, it had been dressed up with banks of flowers and hanging baskets, and a hand-carved sign with gold lettering.

"You've been there?"

"No. My mom's allergic to animals." I shrugged,

remembering how I used to beg her for a pet when we were in the city. Back then she blamed the rules of our apartment building; now it was allergies, which was suspicious since she'd never mentioned them before, but there were certain topics where my mom was completely inflexible and this was one of them. "I love dogs. I wish I could have one."

"There are hypoallergenic breeds."

I was tempted to pretend to be interested just so I'd have an excuse to talk to Jack again. But it was pointless. "Thanks, but I'd have an easier time talking my mom into letting me work as a stripper."

The minute the words were out of my mouth, I felt myself blush furiously, especially when Jack looked me up and down, not bothering to hide the fact that he was checking me out. Which, of course, made me even more self-conscious. Why couldn't I have even a tenth of Rachel's confidence, the ease she had around people?

"So yeah, so I make these things," I babbled, changing the subject. I yanked down the closest piece, a twill jacket to which I'd added purple faux-suede fringe along the outer seams of the sleeves and the bottom hem. The fringe had come from a hideous sofa I'd spotted on the curb in a shabby neighborhood of San Francisco; I'd made my mom pull over so I could take the cushions. The rest of the fabric had been turned into a lampshade as a Mother's Day gift, and my mom had gamely put it in her bedroom, where it looked extremely out of place with all her minimalist modern furniture.

Jack took the jacket from me and ran his hands along the fringe. I was pleased. I loved fabrics that made you want to touch them—textured weaves and lace and silks and embroidery.

"This looks like something you'd wear," he said.

"You just met me!"

"Yeah, but . . . I mean, your style's kind of obvious." Now he did look me up and down, but this time it was my clothes that had his attention.

"I like . . . different stuff, I guess."

"Not many girls could get away with that."

Was that a compliment? I decided to act like it was. "Thanks." I took the jacket back from him and hung it up—anything to do with my hands so I wouldn't have to look at him. "And to answer your question, I mean, you didn't exactly ask a question, but the reason I didn't keep that one is it's too big for me. And purple's more my mom's color."

That wasn't exactly true: *I* knew that purple was her color, with her pale skin and blue eyes and reddish blond hair, but *she* didn't. My mom wore navy and gray and tan, safe colors, colors she could disappear in. I was always trying to talk her into trying something new, but she refused.

"So, are you girls going to chat about fashion all day?" Rachel asked sarcastically. I shot her an exasperated look, wondering why she was brushing Jack off so fast.

"I don't really think when I get dressed." He tugged at his T-shirt, ignoring her. Now that he was closer I could see that it was frayed around the collar. His cargo shorts were shredded along the hem—clearly they'd been washed many, many times.

"Let me guess," I said. "You have your favorites you wear over and over rather than take the time to dig down in the drawer for the ones underneath."

"This is good enough for me. I don't really care how it looks."

"Have you even been in the mall in the last three years?" Rachel asked him.

"Why, so I can drop eighty bucks on a T-shirt covered with graffiti? No thanks."

"You probably don't even know who Earl Dobby is," Rachel retorted.

"Actually, Earl Dobby took his inspiration from the British designers in the sixties," I said. I didn't care for the graffiti look myself, and I didn't hold it against Jack for not knowing—or caring—who Dobby was, even if his designs were selling like crazy in the city. "He's not all that original."

Jack raised an eyebrow, giving me a smile that might have been faintly mocking. "You're serious about this stuff."

"Yes."

"Maybe we should get together so you can tell me more about *fashion* sometime." The emphasis he put on the word made it sound like fashion wasn't at all what he had in mind. Despite the warning bells going off in my brain, I felt myself melt.

"Jesus, leave her alone, Jack," Rachel snapped. "She just

moved here. The last thing she needs is to start hanging out with a freak like you."

Jack just laughed. "Maybe you should let her decide."

"Yes," I said, shooting a glare at Rachel. "I'd love to."

Jack stuck out his hand, and I shook it. It was warm and work-rough and strong, and he held on longer than strictly necessary. At the last minute he pulled me closer, and I brushed against the hem of his T-shirt before he released me.

And caught my breath.

I'd barely touched the soft cotton, but it had been enough to send the silvery static sparkles through my brain, a reaction that signaled a vision. I gasped as the sharp sensation sent shivers down my body, flickering and then disappearing like a TV being turned off. It hadn't lasted long enough for me to see anything, but as I stepped involuntarily back from Jack, I could tell he'd noticed my reaction. His smile went opaque, and his eyes narrowed.

As I turned away from him, I wondered what sort of secrets he was keeping . . . and what bad things he'd done while wearing that shirt.

• • •

We were finished by three, having sold the jeans and quilted bag, the coral jacket—just as Rachel had predicted, a couple of nice ladies from Atherton fell in love with it and even argued over who got to buy it—a sundress I'd embroidered with a retro cross-stitch design, and a skirt with a shredded tulle hem that had been inspired by a photo of Stevie Nicks from the eighties. I'd also taken a commission order, my first—a woman promised to come back the following Saturday with her son's T-shirt collection, which she wanted made into a quilt he could take to college. Even after I turned down her offer of a deposit, we cleared $208.

"So how much are you up to?" Rachel asked, tucking her money into her Coach wristlet.

I did the math in my head. "Around five hundred dollars." Not bad for two weekends.

"So, not a car yet."

"No, Rachel—at least, not a car that would actually work. Even if I had ten times that, I'd be lucky to get a junker without any wheels."

"Maybe you could get *Jack* to fix it for you," she said, an edge to her voice. "Could you have been any more obvious? You were practically climbing into his lap."

"I was not!" We were loading the stand and the unsold things back into Rachel's car, and I took advantage of the task, ducking behind the hatch so Rachel couldn't see my expression. "Is he . . . I mean, does he ever . . ."

"Is he one of us?" Rachel asked as I closed the trunk carefully on the big plastic box. I didn't reply, even though that wasn't exactly what I was trying to ask. I wanted to know if he was trouble, if the vision I'd nearly had was something major, something that should make me keep my distance. "No, definitely not, he's a freak. He moved to Winston in middle school. He's good at sports but he quits every team he's ever on. He's been in a lot of trouble. Like *police* trouble."

"What did he do?"

"I don't know, but does it matter? Seriously, Cee-Cee, you can do so much better."

I knew what Rachel meant by "do better." In Rachel's world, there was her crowd, and everyone else just took up space in the halls of Winston High. I hadn't actually seen her in action at the school yet, but I knew her type—even at Blake we had our own version of a social hierarchy. Vinda Scopes might have had piercings in her lip and cheeks and a shaved head with pink-dyed bangs that hung in her eyes, but she could do mean-girl as well as any suburban queen bee. Most of Vinda's clique were painters, skinny scowling girls who carried their portfolios through the halls without ever deigning to acknowledge any of the other kids, guarding their social prominence and crushing anyone naïve enough to wander into their limelight.

I'd never been one of Vinda's victims, one of the girls you'd see crying in the nook under the stairs after being cut down viciously by her offhand remarks, or discovering her latest attack on Facebook. I had my own friends: Lincoln Cross, who could make me laugh no matter what was going on in my life; Maura Kidder, who once stayed up all night with me helping to fix a hair dye experiment gone horribly wrong; and Caleb Randsome, who I'd met the first day of school when I dropped my tray in the cafeteria line. But I'd also never had any desire to join her circle. I used to like being in the background, more or less invisible, floating from group to group.

Now I wasn't so sure I wanted to remain invisible. I wanted more . . . I wanted what Rachel had. Her confidence, for starters. The ease with which she made friends and became the center of conversation, the way everyone watched her as she walked down the street. But the trouble with my automatic pass into the in crowd at Winston— courtesy of my friendship with her—was that the higher you fly, the farther you fall, and I didn't look forward to crashing to earth when I inevitably screwed up.

It wasn't that I thought Rachel would turn on me or dump me. But even Rachel wouldn't be able to help if the Winston kids decided they didn't think much of a former art-school girl who made her own clothes. If I wasn't careful, I could easily be a freak too.

If I was smart, I'd listen when Rachel tried to steer me in the right social direction. But Jack . . . Well, I wasn't quite ready to let the subject drop. At least not until I knew what the vision had been about.

"Maybe he's just busy," I said. "Turning his life around."

"Cee-Cee." Rachel put a hand on my arm and looked me in the eye. "Like I said, you can do better. I hate to be blunt here, but Jack's only going to drag you down. And trust me, you get just one chance to make a first impression at school. I told you Kane's going to be at the beach tonight, right? He asked me twice if you were planning to be there."

I sighed. I'd seen Kane De Ponceau at the beach the last

two weekends. Six feet three and all of it muscle, he played golf and water polo and lacrosse for Winston. I knew all about it, because he and his friends never got tired of talking about the Wildcats. Apparently their big rivals were Cambria and Monterey High, and at some point in both evenings I'd spent around them, they would do a drunken rendition of the Winston fight song before wandering off to make out with whatever lucky girls they were currently into.

"Oh, be still, my pounding heart," I muttered.

"Okay. I get it. Kane's not your type. How about Luke? He got like a two thousand—something on his SAT. That makes him geeky enough, even for you."

I smiled despite myself. Rachel was a good friend, in her own twisted way. "He's been kicked out of school twice for drugs, according to you."

"They never proved anything." Rachel yawned, stretching her arms luxuriously over her head. "I mean, don't marry him or whatever. It's summer. Come on. You're supposed to be having fun. You can get serious when school starts."

"Yeah," I said, thinking maybe then I could talk to Jack without her giving me a hard time about it.

Rachel shrugged. "Hey, it's your life. I'm just trying to help you be all you can be."

As I got on my bike and started toward home, already sweaty from the hot afternoon sun, I wondered if I could live with the version of me that Rachel was trying so hard to create.

CHAPTER SIX

Mom kept office hours on Saturdays, so she wasn't home yet when I got back to the house. I took a shower and straightened my hair, even though the salty air at the beach would ruin it in ten minutes. At least I'd make a good impression before everyone got too wasted to care.

Taking one of Mom's foil-wrapped pans from the freezer to defrost, I thought about how she had loved to cook when I was little, and was constantly making cakes and muffins and trying new recipes for dinner. But ever since she and my dad split up and she opened her own business, she didn't have time for anything more than the giant batches of stew and casseroles she made every few weeks and froze in two-serving containers. They weren't terrible, but I was sick of having the same meals over and over again. Still, I knew from experience that my criticism would result in her suggesting that I take over the cooking myself. I liked our deal the way it was, with me being responsible for setting the table, defrosting, and cleanup, and her doing the rest, so I kept my mouth shut.

Earlier in the week, Rachel had given me a dress she wanted altered for tonight, and it was waiting in my sewing room. When Mom broke the news that we were moving back to Winston, she promised me I could use the spare bedroom to work on my designs. I'd scavenged used bookshelves and tables to store all my things. My prized possession was Nana's 1982 Bernina Model 930. They don't make sewing machines like it anymore—metal construction, a kick-ass motor, and twenty-six stitches, including the best stretch stitch ever. It didn't do digital embroidery and it didn't have a touch screen, but it never skipped a stitch and could sew through four layers of denim or leather just as easily as featherweight silk. I had taught myself to clean and oil it, and I wouldn't have traded it for the top-of-the-line Husqvarna Viking Sapphire featured in the current edition of *Vogue Sewing*.

I had just positioned the dress inside out on the sewing machine so I could take in the seam when the doorbell rang. I put the presser foot down carefully and went to get the door.

The woman standing on my front porch looked familiar, but I couldn't think of where I'd seen her before. She was in her thirties, with blond hair held back with a headband and a carefully made-up, pleasant face. She was wearing the kind of suit my mom liked, a fitted short-sleeved jacket over a knee-length skirt, except hers was a deep sage green, a shade my mother would never wear.

"Hello," she said brightly. "You must be Clare. I'm Noreen Granger."

Granger. Of course. I kept a smile frozen on my face despite the sickening realization that I was talking to the mother of Dillon Granger, the boy who had been murdered two years ago. "Hi," I said, shaking her hand, which was cool to the touch. "Would you like to come in?"

"Oh, no, I don't want to intrude. I'm just here on behalf of the historic preservation council. I was hoping to talk to your mom for a few minutes. I knew her when we were growing up, though she was a few years ahead of me in school."

"She's at work right now, but I'll let her know that you stopped by. Is there a message you'd like me to give her?"

"Oh, please do, if you would, honey. I wanted to welcome her back to town and invite her to a meeting. We're doing some wonderful work with the town, really focusing on our early history and some of our underutilized resources. We're fund-raising right now for restoration work on the town hall, and we'll have a booth at the Independence Day festival. Will you two be attending?"

I couldn't believe she was out doing volunteer work so close to the anniversary of her son's death, but what did I know? Maybe it helped her to keep busy. Maybe giving her time to the town took her mind off her sadness. "I think so, Mrs. Granger. I'll make sure to suggest we stop by."

"That would be great." She looked around the porch, at the antique wicker furniture, the vase full of sunflowers, the paperback book my mom had left on the table. "I have to admit I have an ulterior motive. We do a house walk every fall, and I'd love to talk your mom into letting us include your house. It has a unique place in Winston history."

I searched her face for irony, but there wasn't any. Maybe the old jokes about the haunting had finally faded away. "That would be fun."

"You're going to love the high school. I can't believe my twenty-year reunion is coming up!" She laughed, revealing a dimple at one corner of her mouth. "What year will you be?"

"Junior."

"Oh, that's too bad. You'd be perfect for Gold Key, you're so darling and smart, but only freshmen are eligible to join. I'm sure you can help on their projects, though—they're always looking for volunteers."

"I'm sure I will." Rachel was a member, and she said there were a lot of boring teas and nursing home visits and holiday caroling, but that anyone who was anyone in Winston was either a present or former member. Her mom had been one but my mom hadn't, and I got the feeling that being excluded had been yet another painful humiliation for her all those years ago.

Nana said it was just a bunch of stuck-up bitches with nothing better to do, and not to worry about it, which made my mom mutter "That's easy for you to say" under her breath, which I actually sympathized with since it's a lot easier not to care about a club that hasn't rejected you.

"Well, I'd be happy to introduce you to some nice families with kids your age, if you like," Mrs. Granger said.

She was so warm and easy to talk to, I spoke without thinking. "We have kind of a reputation in Winston."

She laughed, a genuine, appealing laugh that carried on the breeze. "Oh, you're not talking about that sweet grandmother of yours, are you?"

"Um, yeah," I said, feeling disloyal. "I guess some people wish she'd take better care of her house and all."

Mrs. Granger clucked dismissively. "Don't you listen to them. I adore Lila. She's done so much important work in this town. And when . . . Well, I suppose you know that my husband and I lost our son a while back. Lila wrote me a beautiful letter. I still read it now and then. She's a special lady."

Mrs. Granger hugged me before she left. I put her business card on the kitchen counter, thinking that maybe she and my mom could have coffee or something. Maybe she could become a good friend. She hadn't been at all what I'd expected, but evidently time can heal even the deepest wounds, or at least give you a chance to start living again.

It took just half an hour to alter Rachel's dress. She liked her clothes form-fitting, and I was happy to help, considering everything she had done for me. Besides, it was good practice. I wasn't sure what it said about me that I knew her measurements better than I knew my own, but when I was done with a pair of Rachel's jeans, they fit her like they were painted on.

I'd teased her about wearing a dress to the beach, since

she'd end up in just her bikini within an hour, but Rachel was a big believer in first impressions.

I had chosen my own outfit carefully, too, though I wasn't the beach-dress type. Despite what I'd said to Rachel, I was kind of interested in Luke Herrera, although after meeting Jack I wasn't so sure. I'd taken a walk with Luke once, and it might have even gone farther if one of his friends hadn't thrown a volleyball at us from down the beach, hitting Luke in the back. We stopped kissing just as the last of the sun disappeared below the horizon, its reflection trembling on the surface of the water before it slipped underneath.

The truth was that I'd sort of figured I was heading toward . . . something, with Luke. Maybe even something big. Like, *sleeping with him* big.

It was on my summer to-do list. I mean, not necessarily with Luke, but with someone. I didn't believe in waiting until you were with someone you loved. I wasn't sure I believed in love at all. Or at least, not for me. Things hadn't worked out for my mom, or for my grandmother, who'd already buried two husbands. Nana lost her first husband when my mom was seven. It was a lot tougher back then for single mothers to make a go of it, but Nana always said that was one thing the women of our family were good at—making a go of things.

Ever since I could remember, Nana had dated. Maybe there was something about a free spirit like Nana that was oddly appealing to old men, because she never had any trouble meeting them, despite her sketchy reputation in town. And it wasn't that they left her—*she* tired of *them.* "I'd rather be a tart than a bore," she'd told me more than once during our holiday visits, just one of the many things she said that drove my mother crazy.

My secret fear was that I wasn't cut out even to be a tart. I didn't have . . . *it,* whatever it was. Mom had it, even if she did her best to suffocate it under her boring clothes and soccer mom hair—I saw how men looked at her. Nana had apparently turned down half a dozen marriage proposals after her first husband died before settling on rich old Doyle Raley. But I suspected I wasn't half the head turner either of them was.

Maybe that was why I'd told Rachel all about Lincoln Cross, my best friend at Blake. I'd stretched the truth, saying he wasn't just a friend but my boyfriend. He was a lot more impressive than anyone I'd actually dated, and I told Rachel about how I used to ride behind him on the Suzuki Hayabusa motorcycle his dad gave him when he turned sixteen, the music he wrote, the computer room in his dad's condo with the speakers that cost more than the motorcycle. About his wavy brown hair that came well past his shoulders, and nights up on the roof deck high above their Nob Hill neighborhood. About how Lincoln and I liked to wrap up in a comforter after sex, often falling asleep on the double lounge chair by his dad's koi pond.

Most of which was true. Except that Lincoln's father would have never let him touch the Hayabusa. And instead of sex, it was usually Scrabble. And, um, there was the fact that Lincoln was gay. I told myself these were minor omissions, during those first few days when Rachel and I were getting reacquainted and I needed something—anything—to impress her. . . . And now it was too late to tell her the truth.

Yet. I would tell her the truth, about that and a few other small lies I'd told back when I felt like I was trying to get used to the new life my mother had thrust us into. I just wanted to wait a little longer, cement our friendship, make sure it was really going to *last* before I took that kind of risk. I couldn't afford to lose my one sure thing. The few times I'd spoken to Lincoln since we'd moved, I hadn't told him everything about Rachel and my new life, either. It was like I wasn't sure the two halves would fit together, but I knew I had to own up soon and be honest with both of them.

After I finished Rachel's dress, I pressed it and my own outfit, which was pretty tame by my standards—a plain black tank top and an ancient pair of cutoffs whose pockets I'd appliquéd with the logos from antique flour sacks. I'd beaded my flip-flops myself, and I had a necklace I'd made by drilling holes in coins Nana had brought back from a trip to India and stringing them on a silk ribbon along with black glass beads.

Mom still wasn't home, so I put the casserole in the oven and opened the box of old clothes I stored in my room. I'd bought some of them at a tag sale the week before, and the rest I'd found on the porch. Word had gotten around town about my business, and people had started leaving me old clothes and quilts, even tablecloths and dish towels. Everyone—friends of my mom, kids I'd met through Rachel, neighbors along San Benito Road—thought of me when they had things they didn't want anymore, and I got some good things that way. But I still went to garage sales and junk sales and flea markets, because I loved old things, vintage pieces full of personality, things you couldn't find today.

At the top of the box was a plastic bag stuffed with clothes that I'd bought from a dazed-looking woman in a baseball cap. She had been sitting behind a card table in a vacant lot at the edge of town along with half a dozen other vendors. I didn't know where they had found the things they sold at their hard-luck flea market, but every week their broken-down cars and ancient trucks were loaded with junk—mismatched dishes and tarnished silver and water-stained books, blankets and toys and lamps that had seen better days. I went through piles of clothes without seeing anything special, but then I saw a plastic bag labeled "Odds and Ends $5." I could see a brown suede garment through the plastic, probably a skirt. I had no doubt that it was either ruined, ripped, stained, or burnt, but I knew I could cut it apart and use it anyway, and that was worth five dollars no matter what else was in the bag.

I dumped the contents onto the carpeted floor, and colorful pieces tumbled out: a paisley polyester blouse and a pair of striped tights with a long run in them.

A denim jacket with a cropped hem and distressed silver buttons caught my eye. It was badly stained and wrinkled, with dirt ground into the seams, and there was a rip in one sleeve. The label read "Ripley Couture," an expensive brand I'd seen in a San Francisco boutique. The jacket had to have cost several hundred dollars, and I wondered how it had ended up in the flea market, especially in this condition. It was too damaged to be salvaged, but the buttons were pretty, and I knew I'd find a use for them. In the time it took for my hand to reach for the jacket, I'd already decided to try them with a seventies-era jumper I was working on—

A powerful tremor shattered my synapses, jerking my thoughts violently. I cried out. I think I did, anyway. The fabric was alive in my hands, sending silvery sparks rocketing through my body into my mind, exploding with pain.

It had never been this strong before.

I couldn't let go. My fingers were frozen around the fabric, and my other senses faded away. All that remained were the flashes and the sparks and a sudden burning heat that radiated out from my heart to my fingertips. I waited, struggling to keep breathing, because I knew what would come next.

I held the jacket in my hands, unable to let go, waiting for the painful tremor to run its course. Finally it fell from my trembling fingertips into a heap on the floor. I crawled away from it, forcing myself to calm down. The shortness of breath, the pain behind my eyes—these felt real, but they were illusions too, just like the visions.

It's not real, I whispered to myself. Technically, it was true—the denim jacket was only a garment, an inanimate thing that was bound by the same physical laws as every other object in the house. Gravity made it fall to the floor;

invisible air currents lifted and fluttered the collar. The shade of blue, I knew from my color theory class at Blake, was a product of light refraction, no more real than concepts like virtue or destiny.

"You're not real," I told the jacket, but I still felt its tug. I felt like I wouldn't be able to leave it alone until I understood the vision, what it was trying to tell me.

My bedroom carpet was soft and soothing under my hands and knees. Never had my visions altered the physical world—no garment had ever wrapped itself around my wrist or throat; no zipper had scraped itself against my flesh. The sparkles I felt were not temperature or sensation—they were not of any sense I could name, other than the connection I felt to others' lives.

But this time had been different. Moments earlier, the tremor had shocked me, rocked me, thrown me from my axis. Left me gasping, as though if I hadn't let go, it would have consumed me. Taken me.

Ended me.

Stupid, I chided myself at the unbidden words. I was being overly dramatic and ridiculous, the result of anxiety about the evening ahead. I'd been high-strung all afternoon because of the encounter with Hoff, the thrill of selling so many items, the . . . whatever it was with Jack. And like every Saturday night, I fretted over getting dressed, over what I would say, how much I would drink, how I would hide it from my mom, whether this would finally be the night Rachel realized I was nothing but a liability.

That was all it was. Overreacting by an epic overreactor.

My drama skills, forged at the legendary Blake School, were unmatched in this sleepy town. All I had to do was get ahold of myself. Break it down. Think it through.

What exactly had I felt when I touched the cotton fabric? I closed my eyes and concentrated, teasing apart the emotions until I could identify them individually. *Terror, dismay, grief.* Okay. I felt milder variations of those every day. Well, every week, anyway. What teenage girl didn't?

But there had been something else. . . . I replayed the scene that had fast-forwarded through me along with the jolt, searching for the details among the confusion. *The sensation of being thrown sideways, a sharp pain as my knee struck something, a second impact, a lurching stop. A face—wide eyes and grimace, briefly familiar—a quick vein of . . . could it be relief? And then—*

My fingers closed on the fabric again, my arm reaching for the jacket almost of its own accord, and I was rocketed back into the vision, the sucking vortex of a sense-memory stronger than any other, a hole in the earth that opened to a chasm with no bottom, a wicked blade that grew sharper as it cleaved. All these things were true in that moment, and if I knew—somewhere, deep down where my mortal heart still beat and my veins still carried blood—that this wasn't real, my mind skipped over that knowledge and entered the other surreal place, a place of darkness and fear.

My throat closed up tight, immobilized by the images that had taken hold of me. They were more powerful than my own instincts, stronger than my sense of self-preservation. The urge to resist faded, lost in my swirling battle. I needed to breathe but couldn't be bothered. Black stars splatted against the silver sparkle like fat raindrops, obliterating, obscuring, making me forget, making me start to not care. My fingers trembled and clenched, and then relaxed, angry no more, barely twitching.

I pulled the jacket closer, using both my hands now, shoving the fabric under my chin. It seemed inexplicably silky and I rubbed it against my skin as though it were infused with precious oils, rare scents. The faraway voice of reason whispered weakly that I should be casting the thing away, disposing of it, burning it—and still I could not stop.

"Youuuuu," a different, stronger voice said. A voice thick with fury, desperation, anguish. A face, its features blurred, contorted and twisted with pain, and I recoiled from it, but I couldn't move. . . . Somewhere, in another place and time, I knew that my fingers clutched the jacket and couldn't let go. But that reality was fading rapidly as the face regarded me with hatred, barely more than an outline, the details shimmering and fading in a cascade of the silver sparks. I didn't know why this entity despised me so much.

This was different from other visions I'd had. Usually they were like old-fashioned films, frame after frame from the past whirring by, events in which the wearer had participated, damage he or she had caused, wrongs committed. I'd heard voices before, but it was rare. This one felt more personal. Somewhere, a person's rage was so strong that it could be transported through the medium of the jacket, had managed to travel the same dark path as the visions, to speak to me this way.

My mind danced between what it knew and these borrowed memories, blurring them together until the terror became my own. My fear was deep and raw, a fear for my very life. Something—someone—wanted to harm me, and unless I did something to stop them, they would succeed. But at the same time I felt . . . pity. And guilt. I had done something to deserve this; I had played a part in whatever horror had transpired. But what had I done? The memories eluded me with maddening, quicksilver speed, disappearing just as I thought I was about to understand.

The face came closer, snarling and spitting, wailing, taking up the entire screen of my inner eye, brandishing itself across the expanse of my mind. Hands . . . The face was no longer disembodied; a shadow figure raised its arms toward me, reaching, threatening, longing to hurt me, strike me, strangle me. Agonizing tremors wracked me even while I knew my mortal body was locked in place, immobile, helpless. It felt as though the vision would somehow cross over, as though its rage was strong enough to defeat the thin barrier between the remembered and the real and find a way to hurt me from deep within my mind.

"You know why."

The voice hissed at me, wrecked and broken, and I could make out teeth and bared lips. And I did know why—or not why, exactly, only that I deserved what was coming.

A fist swung toward me. Sharp pain. Flickering light. Everything rushing away.

Then nothing.

CHAPTER SEVEN

I WASN'T OUT LONG. When I came to, I was lying on the carpet in the middle of the room, the sun streaming in at an angle as it slipped lower toward evening. The oven timer was going off, and I vaguely remembered the casserole. The denim jacket lay inches from my outstretched hand, a stray thread trailing from the cuff seam.

It looked perfectly innocent now, but I wasn't taking any chances. I stuffed all the other clothes back into the box, and then I went to the kitchen. After taking out the casserole and turning off the oven, I dug into the utensil drawer for a pair of tongs and took them back to my room. I stood over the jacket and took a deep breath, feeling ridiculous. But if the thing worked so strongly on me, maybe there was a chance it would work through the metal and plastic of the tongs, and if so, I wanted to be ready to drop them rather than endure the vision again.

Let go, I whispered to myself, just in case. The visions seemed to paralyze me, or at least prevent me from moving on my own; but if I knew in advance—if I was ready—surely I could overcome that.

Slowly, cautiously, I reached the tongs toward the jacket and, holding my breath, prodded the denim fabric. Nothing. I let my breath out in a sigh of relief, gingerly picking up the jacket and dropping it into the cardboard box. When no fabric protruded over the edges, I jammed the top down on the box and then, for good measure, got the tape from the junk drawer and taped it shut.

I sat cross-legged next to it for a moment, trying to figure out what to do next. I could walk outside to the garbage bin, upend the clothes into it, and in two days the trash truck would haul them away and I'd never have to deal with the jacket again. Yes. I could be free of this confusing vision; whatever bad deeds had been done by the person who wore the jacket were in the past, and nothing I could do would change that.

It was an old excuse, one I brought out whenever I didn't want to act on my visions, which was most of the time. Nana had told me, all those years ago, that I wasn't required to do anything at all, and that if I didn't, the visions would slowly disappear. But I hadn't always let that happen. Occasionally, I stepped in.

When I was thirteen, I touched one of my mom's clients' coats and saw a vision of a woman going through a medicine cabinet, stuffing bottles into her purse. It was years before I understood that she was stealing drugs to support a habit, so I hadn't said anything.

But the next year, when I had a vision of one of the boys

in our building shoplifting candy from the little convenience store down the block, I told the proprietor.

When I had a vision of a girl in my chemistry class stealing the exam key, I left an anonymous note for the teacher.

I was learning something about myself—that I could not always resist trying to bring justice to those who might get away undetected.

I had always suspected that was the point of the visions. It was true that our strange gift had been born in the midst of violence and bloodshed; my great-great-grandmother's death had been avenged when her killer was executed, but now I believed that her descendants were meant to right other wrongs too. Even minor ones. Even the ones that didn't have obvious victims. The visions seemed to be giving me the chance to change things in the future.

But this time was different. I didn't want this . . . communication. Or curse. Or whatever it was. But now it had found me. It wanted something from me. The individual in the denim jacket had done something. Maybe something *really* bad. The possibilities spun through my mind. . . .

But that was ridiculous. Winston was a small town, and whatever passed for news made the rounds within hours. When one of Mom's clients, a patent attorney, got a DWI, everyone knew by the next morning. When the town council voted to approve a second Starbucks, protestors had mobilized by lunchtime.

There had been no new tragedies in Winston since last summer. Whatever the owner of the jacket had done, it hadn't been bad enough to make the news. The visions must be mistaken, or exaggerated, or I was misinterpreting them, and I could get rid of the thing with a clear conscience.

Except.

I couldn't forget the face, the terrible expression of pain and fury, the sensations I'd relived. Something bad had happened. And here, in the box, was the evidence. Even if I decided I could ignore all that, I had a feeling the jacket wasn't about to let me.

With a feeling that I would regret it, I carried the box to my room and shoved it into the back of my closet—just as I heard the front door.

I met Mom in the kitchen going through the mail, her big sunglasses pushed up on top of her head.

"Hey, Clare-Bear," she said absently. I winced at the old nickname, one I thought she'd finally forgotten. "God, what a day. Want to go get a pizza, forget all our troubles for a while?"

"Mom—it's *Saturday*. I'm busy tonight."

She blinked, raising her eyebrows, and really focused on me. "Oh. Are you sure?"

"Uh . . . yeah."

"It's just that . . . wow. The days have kind of been running together. That MacGregor audit is killing me—and he was in today, brought me *that*." She pointed to the leather bag she took with her everywhere; it was overflowing with file folders and binders. "He hasn't filed his expenses in five *years*."

You'd think that after being an accountant for two

63

decades, my mom would be used to clients whose record-keeping left a lot to be desired. And they were her best customers, anyway, the ones who paid extra for over-time, whose accounts clocked the endless hours that paid the bills.

I had thought Mom would be happier as her own boss, but now I wasn't so sure. She was working even longer hours, meeting with all the firm's clients to transition them over. So much for her promises to slow down, stress less, reconnect with her old life. And I was getting tired of it.

"Sorry," I said, without much sympathy. "But I'm going to the beach tonight. Remember?"

Mom wrinkled her nose and frowned. "Don't you guys ever do anything besides hang out at that beach? When I was in high school, we wouldn't have been caught dead there at night."

You didn't have any friends, I thought, but I didn't say it. "You should be glad. It's *free.*"

"Yes, except for the three swimsuits you bought this year alone and the sandals you had to replace after you lost the ones that were practically brand-new and the sunglasses that, I should point out, we could have gotten at Target for a tenth of what you paid—"

"*Mom.*" I hated when she did this—she could get herself completely wound up in seconds when it came to money. Ever since Dad stopped sending the support payments, she'd become completely obsessed. It wasn't like I wanted to defend my dad—he'd recently forgotten my birthday for the second year in a row—but he *had* given us his half of the house, which I knew was worth a lot of money. "I bought those myself, remember? With money I *earned*?"

Mom glared at me, her nostrils flaring, a sure sign she was working herself up again. The sunglasses were a sore point, but I couldn't exactly live in a beach town, where I wore them every single day, and not get a decent pair. Besides, it was Mom who was always drilling it into me that it was better to spend money on a few good pieces than buy every trend. Well, she used to say that, anyway, before I started making most of my clothes from thrift-shop finds.

"Yes. All right. I'm sorry." She flashed me a brief smile. "I'm beat anyway. I think that staying in tonight's just what I need." She patted her tote bag, where I knew a paperback was buried under all those folders—Mom never went anywhere without a romance novel.

I almost felt sorry for her. She hadn't been on a date in a couple of years, or even out with friends since we moved back to Winston. She was still pretty, despite her efforts to hide it with her boring haircut and clothes, but she was getting deeper and deeper into a rut, doing nothing but working and sleeping.

But that was *her* choice. I knew there were a dozen people she could call, right here in town. When I was little, she used to take me to a playgroup with a bunch of moms she'd gone to high school with, including Rachel's. Why couldn't she be normal and play Bunco or host jewelry parties like all the other moms and just leave me alone?

"Mom . . . have you called any of those old friends of yours?"

She turned away from me, lifting the foil on the casserole cooling on the counter, poking at the steaming contents. "A couple . . . I might have coffee with my old tennis partner next week."

"What about Mrs. Slade? Weren't you guys going to do a girls' night?"

Mom gave me a funny look, one I couldn't interpret. In the time we'd been back, I'd seen Rachel's mom almost as much as I saw my own, since she didn't work and was always around the house when we hung out there. I remembered her and my mom drinking coffee and talking when Rachel and I were little. But as far as I knew they'd barely seen each other since we moved back. Rachel couldn't explain it either.

"I'm sure we will," Mom said evasively. "As soon as things settle down."

I thought about pointing out that it didn't get a whole lot more settled than a middle-aged woman spending her Saturday night with a romance novel and a bowl of ice cream. But in the end, a desire to keep the peace—or at least stay out of trouble so I could go to the beach—won out.

"Oh," I said, remembering the card on the counter. "Mrs. Granger stopped by. Dillon's mom?"

My mother looked up, surprised. "You're kidding. What did she want?"

My irritation spiked again. "Jeez, Mom, calm down. She was being *friendly*. Something you could maybe learn from her. She wanted to talk to you about the historical society, about putting our house on the house walk this fall."

"Really." Mom's voice dripped with sarcasm. "So that everyone in town can walk through here and whisper about ghosts and your crazy grandmother? No thanks."

Even though that had been exactly my first reaction, coming from Mom it made me mad. "You know what, maybe you should give her a chance and not just assume everyone's out to get you. So you were a loser in high school—that was decades ago. I mean, Mrs. Granger lost her *child* and she's still making an effort."

Mom's look of wounded surprise meant I'd won this round. But as I left the room, her silence wasn't nearly as satisfying as I'd expected it to be.

• • •

"I have a surprise," Rachel said as we walked down the twisting path to the beach, dragging a wheeled cooler behind us. She had just changed into the dress I'd tailored for her, and it fit her perfectly.

The north end of Black Rock Beach was sheltered by cliffs that the tide had carved out of the shore. The rock face wasn't really black—it was a mottled gray—but when it was wet, it looked black and kind of spooky. The beach below was one of the best for miles, sheltered by the cliffs from the wind, the sand pebbled with shells and bits of sea treasure. During the day it was crowded with families, picnickers, and sun worshippers. In theory the beach closed at sunset—signs announcing that rule were posted at the top of the path—but with the California government being so broke, it was cutting services left and right, and the cops never patrolled the beach at night. In the half dozen times I'd been there, we'd never been visited by the police.

It helped that the place where we built our bonfires was shielded from view by the curve of the cliffs. Mom had been worried about safety, and even threatened to talk to the other parents about setting up some sort of patrol rotation to make sure we weren't venturing into the water or walking along the rocky overhang in the dark. Common sense won out when I asked her if she really thought I would mess up the hair it took me half an hour to straighten, and she agreed to leave me alone if I stuck to the curfew.

"Let me guess," I said. "Does it come in a bottle with a Dell Market sticker?"

Everyone knew that the Dell Market had a company-wide no-chase policy—meaning that if a shoplifter made it out the front door, they were home free. Inside the store, you were dead if they caught you, but because of liability or something, they forbid their employees from chasing anyone who got past the doors.

I still thought it was a pretty stupid risk to take, but some of the guys had made stealing liquor into a competitive sport. Last week one of them got two forty-dollar bottles of champagne. Generally, though, they went for the high-proof stuff, hiding a bottle of vodka or rum under their baggy shorts, and the girls' job was to bring the ice, mixers, and snacks. I'd gotten stuck being the designated driver tonight, so I didn't care what they'd managed to snag.

"No! All that's in here is water and soda. Swear!" Rachel

flashed me her innocent smile, the one that had her parents convinced she was up to nothing more than a little wholesome fun. Rachel was an incredible actress, but her real asset was her willingness to go the extra distance to keep that image: it wasn't for nothing that she kept her grades up and showed up for every Gold Key project and sang in the youth choir at her church—all these were worth it, according to Rachel, to keep peace with her mom.

Mrs. Slade hadn't just been a member of the Gold Key Society, she'd been its president. She'd also been valedictorian and president of the Winston High student council, facts that she was constantly holding over Rachel's head. To outside appearances, Rachel was an outstanding kid. But she'd hinted in the past that it was never enough for her mother, who expected her to excel at everything. In Mrs. Slade's mind, Rachel should have been *captain* of the cheer squad, bringing home perfect grades and probably saving the world in her spare time. I couldn't imagine what it must be like to live with that kind of pressure—and I sometimes wondered privately if that was the source of Rachel's occasional recklessness, which she managed to hide from everyone but her closest friends.

"Okay, let's think," I said. "Hmm, you're going to invite me to be part of a threesome."

Rachel laughed. I had learned that the best defense against her bad-girl side was a good offense; as long as I played along, she didn't give me a hard time. "I hadn't thought of that. Let's see, who should we get?"

"Nobody around here," I said, with feeling. The truth

was that I was having doubts about my plan to have casual sex with *one* guy at a time, much less two, but it was easier to pretend that I just wasn't interested in any of them.

"I know, right? And that's why . . ."

Rachel's voice trailed off as we took the final hairpin turn in the path and reached the beach. Eight or ten kids were already gathered around the fire pit, trying to get the fire started.

Including Jack.

He was wearing a clean T-shirt and the shorts he'd had on earlier in the day, but he'd been in the water—the shirt was plastered to his chest and arms. Giselle Dollson wasn't even bothering to hide the fact that she was staring, and Jenna Liu was standing too close, curling her hair around her finger as she talked to him.

Figures. The day I discovered a guy I might actually like, everyone else in town discovered him too.

"I thought you said he didn't hang out," I said.

Rachel frowned. "He doesn't. I'm not sure what he's doing here." She sounded irritated. "The surprise was that I told Ky and Luke to leave their stupid Frisbee at home. Thought you and Luke might finally get a little time to yourselves."

"What did you do?" I demanded, heart sinking.

"Just texted him. Nothing! Don't get all weird about it."

I found Luke in the crowd, tossing Fritos into the air and catching them in his mouth. He missed about half the time. I had a feeling Jack Dimaunahan didn't have a lot in common with the rest of the guys here, but before I could dwell on it, Rachel let out a whoop and ran straight into the clump of kids. At the last moment Ky picked her up and carried her to the water's edge, pretending to throw her in, while I did my usual last-minute pep talk and tried to convince myself that this time I'd actually be able to relax enough to have fun.

CHAPTER EIGHT

RELAXING WAS HARDER THAN USUAL TONIGHT, given what had happened with the denim jacket and the presence of Jack, who turned out to be pretty good at volleyball. He and a few of the other guys split into teams, switching to a glow-in-the-dark ball when night fell. He had a wicked serve, and every time he spiked, the ball crashed down onto the sand on the other side of the net, guys falling on the ball a split second too late. I noticed the way his team moved back to give him space.

I wasn't the only girl who watched, but I was the only one with my own personal bartender. "Okay, okay," I protested the fourth time Rachel filled my plastic cup with Diet Coke, adding rum to her own cup. "But unless you want me to float away, how about you slow down?"

"Sorry, I'm going off the clock." Rachel laughed and, true to her word, she disappeared with Ky. Apparently Hopper had been given the bad news that he was being dumped—Rachel had been thinking of breaking up with him for a while—and Ky wasn't about to let his friendship with Hopper get in the way of a chance with Rachel.

I sipped my soda and talked to Jenna and Lara Prytowsky and Victoria Abelson—actually, I mostly listened, enjoying the sound of their laughter, the salty air on my skin, and the cool night breeze. I had hoped to have some time alone with Rachel tonight; I was thinking about telling her about the jacket. But first I'd have to tell her about my visions. I had thought that after she had a drink or two it might be easier for me to tell her—and maybe easier for her to hear it—but I hadn't gotten my nerve up before the party got into full swing and it was too late.

I wanted to trust my friendship with Rachel, but something was keeping me teetering on the edge. Occasionally she got quiet and seemed to retreat into her thoughts. Sometimes she snapped at me for no reason. It wasn't just me—I'd seen her do it to her other friends, too, and she could be impatient with Adrienne. She could also be really sweet, and most of the time she was upbeat and positive. Her dark moods were so dark, though, it sometimes worried me.

For the thousandth time I found myself missing Lincoln, and I promised myself I'd call him soon. I'd been so busy with my life that I hadn't talked to him in over a week. He had a few flaws as a best friend—chief among them that he had no interest in clothes or fashion—but he was a good listener and I knew I could trust him. Rachel had never done anything to make me regret sharing my thoughts with her, but she wasn't an open book the way Lincoln was.

And what would happen if she ever figured out that I wasn't cool enough for this crowd after all?

As if reading my thoughts, Lara leaned over and touched the hem of my shorts, smoothing out the ragged fringe. "You always look soooo amazing," she said in the dreamy voice of someone who'd been drinking a lot. "You have, like, *real* style. Not like, you know, everyone else's style. But real. You're *real*. On the inside. Where it really counts."

For emphasis Lara tapped on her chest and sighed, staring into my eyes like she was about to hug me. She was wearing a tight, cropped red and white striped tank top with a white star appliqué on the chest, and as her fingertips brushed the star I remembered that there would be fireworks over this very beach three nights from now to cap off the big festival.

Luke and Hopper, who'd been making a beer run to the coolers, dropped to the sand next to us.

"Oh, Jesus, are you guys gonna make out?" Hopper demanded drunkenly. "Oh, shit, that's so hot."

Lara giggled and put her hand on my shoulder. "Hopper! I'm totally straight. But if I wasn't . . ."

I'd seen this before, girls flirting with each other, mostly for the guys' amusement. None of these girls were bi, that I knew of, not in this crowd. Lincoln had a theory that everyone experimented by the time they got out of college—he even had a list of straight guys he hoped to catch during their experimental phase—but somehow I doubted that Winston High was quite as progressive as the Blake School. As for me, the thought of kissing a girl wasn't appealing.

But tonight was different. Everything was so beautiful—the inky sky full of stars, the glimmer of moonlight out on the water, the laughter of my friends. Somewhere nearby, I had a new best friend, someone who cared about me and who I would have all kinds of fun with in my last two years of high school. I was feeling funny and clever and happy, even if I wasn't drinking—what would it hurt to play along, to have a little fun tonight?

I put my arm around Lara and leaned against her shoulder. She smelled nice, like spicy perfume and rum, and she giggled and hugged me back. As my hand slid down her back and rested on the fabric of her top, the energy inside me hitched and bucked and reversed, the pleasant moment being sucked backward toward a swirling vortex, a voice shrilling over a thick blanket of pain.

Take your hand away, I willed myself. Ordinarily I would never have my defenses down when I touched someone—it had become second nature to me to steel myself. I tried to resist the visions, or at least control them. But tonight everything seemed possible, and I hesitated, enjoying being part of the crowd, part of this group of pretty girls who seemed to take all their good fortune for granted. I liked feeling popular. I liked feeling wanted.

But as my hand rested on her back, I sensed . . . something. And still I didn't pull away. Lara's memories, her emotions and thoughts, flowed through my fingertips and flickered to life in my mind, and I had barely absorbed her brittle cheer before I felt it break into a thousand shards against the sadness that lay just below the surface.

Once it began, it was too late to break away, to interrupt the transfer. I let myself go, the energy flowing through her shirt into my hand, along my nerves and veins to my mind and heart, and the cool sand fell away beneath me, the starry sky disappeared above me, and I was inside Lara's mind. It was an anxious place.

In the vision, Lara—her hair longer, and not as blond— was walking along the liquor aisle of a grocery store. I knew it had to be Dell Market even before I recognized the well-stocked refrigerators full of sodas and beers, the bakery cases at the end of the aisle. Where else would a couple of high school girls go to steal liquor?

Sure enough, in the vision, Lara was accompanied by another girl. I saw her from the back, her long hair cascading over her shoulders as she bent down like she was considering the bottles of carbonated juice stocked on the lowest shelves of the refrigerator. Her hands moved over the bottles, and as she picked one up and looked at it, I saw a flash of her profile, her high cheekbones and lips curved in a smile.

But I knew she was covering for Lara, who chatted and turned her back on the shelves behind her, even as her hand reached behind and her fingers closed around the neck of a bottle of premium vodka. Her eyes were bright, but as she giggled I recognized the faint anxiety that seemed to be a permanent part of her. I'd heard rumors that her stepfather was mean, that she was moving up to Oregon with her older sister as soon as she graduated.

I watched Lara slide the bottle into the big leather handbag she had slung over her shoulder, heard the clank of glass against glass, and knew that she'd already stolen another bottle. The vision had to be from a year ago; Lara must have picked out the red, white, and blue top for a holiday weekend beach party much like this one, then put it away in the bottom of a drawer until July came around again. Lara was a thief, along with her pretty friend, and as my hand rested on her back, the cotton fabric told me all about the guilt she carried with her.

A couple of stolen bottles of alcohol—that wasn't so bad, was it? Nothing lots of other kids hadn't done. Nothing I had to do anything about, anyway. It was no business of mine. As the vision faded, the pieces spinning and shattering, replaced by the salty breeze and the flickering light of the moon over the water, I breathed in deeply and let it out, trying to pretend I didn't know this new thing about a girl who I'd hoped would be my friend.

There was something I was missing, something that nagged at the edges of my mind. There was more to what I'd seen than a couple of girls stealing liquor, but I couldn't quite get hold of it. The pleasant mood from moments before had disappeared, replaced with a throbbing headache and faint nausea, the occasional aftereffects of a vision. At least it was nothing like the reaction I'd had earlier, the one that had left me facedown on my bedroom floor. I'd never had two visions in one day before, and it was exhausting.

"Come on," Hopper was chanting. "Kiss her. With tongue. You know you'll like it."

I pulled away from Lara, who uttered a wobbly "Hey" and smiled uncertainly at me. I managed to get to my feet as Hopper muttered something I couldn't understand and Luke lurched drunkenly to his feet, asking if I was okay.

"Yeah, just—I think I need to get some air. Maybe walk."

"I'll come with you."

A few days ago this was exactly what I'd been hoping would happen, that Luke would ask me to walk along the beach again, that we might end up making out on the sand this time, and maybe going somewhere in his car after. Down the road a few miles was a scenic lookout where kids went to park—but the smart ones drove an extra ten minutes, taking a dirt road up to *another* lookout, where the cops didn't come by to make sure people weren't having sex or getting high.

I had no intention of getting high. But in my purse, wrapped in tissue and stuffed in the bottom of my makeup bag, was one of the condoms my mother had insisted on keeping stocked in the linen closet since I turned thirteen. It was just in case—Mom had been preaching "just in case" forever—but I had been well on the way to convincing myself that Luke was the one, until I met Jack.

Now I wasn't so sure. So much had happened today, and between the filthy torn jacket and the thing with Lara, I'd experienced two powerful visions. Every vision left me feeling tingly and light-headed, but these last two were different. They seemed somehow more directed at me, more . . . urgent. Certainly, they were physically more painful and exhausting. And I couldn't help thinking that they were linked, that they were leading to something that had happened in this town, something I was supposed to do something about. The trouble was, I had no idea what. I only knew that after this last vision I felt nauseated and weak and about to cry.

"I'm good," I forced myself to say, with a grin that probably wasn't very convincing. Between the moonlight and the streetlights high above, I could make out the confusion on Luke's face. "Maybe in a while," I added, "after I walk a little."

"What do you mean, in a while? Let's go now." He threw an arm around my shoulders, and I could smell the liquor on his breath. It wasn't hard to duck out of his grip, even as he tried to grab my arm. "Hey! C'mere!"

"Sorry, Luke, I think I want to be by myself right now."

He muttered something that sounded a lot like "goddamn tease," and as I started down the beach, I was glad I'd turned him down. I'd thought he was a pretty good guy when he wasn't drinking, but any interest I'd had in him was gone.

I watched the moon glimmering far out over the ocean, a pale yellow globe whose reflection danced on the water. The ocean was so beautiful here. I'd taken it for granted in San Francisco. I took off my flip-flops and felt the sand on my feet, soft and damp and cool. The sounds of the party grew fainter behind me, and seagulls hoping for a handout wheeled and screeched above, finally giving up and going wherever they go to sleep at night.

"Hey, Clare."

I turned to see someone jogging toward me. For a moment I thought it was Luke, but then I saw the outline of his long hair: Jack.

"Hi," I said, waiting for him. A wave came farther up the beach, covering my feet, making them sink into the sand.

"What'd you say to Luke?"

"Nothing. I just didn't want to walk with him." Jack stood close enough that I could see the moon reflected in his eyes. "He called me a tease."

"Are you?"

I was so stunned by his question that I didn't answer. I felt both offended and intrigued, because I didn't think that was what he was really asking me.

"Whatever," Jack said, when I didn't answer. "But look. You should stay out of the water."

I bristled at his tone. I didn't like being told what to do. Mom had given me a lot of freedom—but I liked to think I'd earned it, keeping my grades up and following most of her rules. I'd never been in any trouble at school, but then again, you'd have to do something really spectacular at Blake to get in trouble, since they prided themselves on having such a creative—read *permissive*—atmosphere.

"I'm not *drunk*."

"Didn't say you were. Still, it's not a great idea to be in

the water by yourself in the dark. People die on the coast every summer."

"People died right here in Winston the last two summers."

Jack laughed unexpectedly, a bitter, soulless sound. "Fine. Suit yourself."

He started to walk away from me and I didn't want him to go. "Wait. Jack."

"Listen, I'm not your babysitter. Do whatever you want."

"No, it's not that. I'm sorry. Can we—can we start over?"

For a minute he paused, and I saw him in silhouette against the glow of the far-off bonfire. Broad shoulders. Those ridiculous shredded shorts. Hair blowing in the breeze. Hands clenched into fists . . . slowly relaxing.

He turned back to me, his expression unreadable. "My dad volunteered in the fire department. He pulled people out of the water, did search and rescue, all that. Know what he gave me on my tenth birthday?"

"What?"

"A bunch of pictures of motorcycle and bike accidents where the victims weren't wearing their helmets. Not pretty, lots of brains on pavement."

"Wow." I swallowed; the image wasn't doing much for my unsettled stomach. Still, I was feeling better otherwise; my head had stopped pounding and the dizziness had faded. "Bet you felt ripped off."

"Maybe. Or maybe he saved my life."

There was a gruffness to Jack's voice that was hard to read.

"Well. He sounds . . . like a concerned dad."

"He was."

Was?

I knew I should say something, but in my wobbly state the moment passed while I was clumsily trying to find the words, and then I was just standing there feeling stupid, wondering if Jack's dad had died or just left, like mine. Although fathers who took the time to worry about their kids' safety didn't strike me as the kind who left. My own father had barely paid any attention to me when he lived with us, and once he was gone, it was like he forgot about me. For my tenth birthday, my dad had sent me a princess costume that might have fit a five-year-old, and a card in which he wrote that he'd call soon. Which had kept me going for a while, because back then I still believed his promises.

"So, you want to walk some more?" He had already set out down the beach ahead of me, and I had to race to catch up.

"Um, sure." I tried to think of what we could talk about; Jack didn't exactly invite conversation. "Did you try those hard lemonades Ky brought?"

"I don't drink."

"Oh. You don't?" I was barely managing two or three words at a time.

"Or smoke. Or anything."

"Is it because of soccer?"

"No. I'm quitting the team." He paused, then seemed to relent. "It's no big deal. I partied a lot, for a while. After my dad died. I didn't like what it did to me."

"I'm really sorry," I said. "How long ago was it . . . I mean, did it happen in a fire?"

"No. He was an electrician. There was an accident at a job site." Jack spoke without any emotion, hands jammed in his pockets.

"I'm so sorry," I repeated, feeling stupid. I shouldn't have asked. "I don't know what I'd do if anything happened to my mom."

"It's okay. I was messed up for a while, but my uncle beat the shit out of me after I got in trouble a few times."

"And that was . . . a good thing?"

"Kept me from getting worse. He went to school and talked to my guidance counselor and they worked something out. Suddenly I was working at the clinic after school."

"Is that why you don't hang out with everyone? Because you're always working?"

"Who told you I don't hang out with them?"

I could feel myself blush. I was going to kill Rachel. "I only meant . . . I haven't seen you around. At the beach."

"Your crowd parties a *lot*."

I couldn't tell if I detected judgment in his voice—or a warning. "They're not my crowd," I said defensively.

His laugh was the same as before—abrupt and bitter. "Yeah? Seems like you're always around Rachel."

"Rachel's not what you think."

"How do you know what I think?"

I couldn't help it—I was stung by his tone. "What about the rest of them? You hate everyone? Is that it?"

Jack rolled his eyes, and ticked off a list on his fingers.

"Rick and Ky are on the soccer team. Hopper's been in my Spanish class since middle school. Luke lives a couple of blocks from me; we both got suspended from school in ninth grade for jumping the fence to chase a coyote at recess. I don't have anything against any of them."

I wanted to ask him how well he knew all the girls, too—I was thinking of the way Jenna had looked at him. Maybe that was it—maybe *Rachel* liked him. I'd never seen a guy turn her down, but maybe Jack had, and now she couldn't stand him.

"Can I ask you something?" It seemed important to figure this one out, since it involved my best friend and the only guy in Winston I'd found myself attracted to. "What's the real reason you don't like Rachel?"

"Nothing, really. She's . . . popular. I'm just surprised that you and she have anything in common. How do you know her, anyway? Didn't you just move here?"

I wondered if I should be offended. "Our moms were in a playgroup together when we were little—Rachel and I were very close until I moved away. We kept in touch."

"You used to live here?"

"Yeah, Rachel didn't tell you that?"

"No. Makes me wonder what else I don't know about you."

Somehow, we had stopped walking. Jack put his hand on my arm, turning me toward him.

And then he kissed me.

I'd made out with a few boys. There was Dan Schwermer, a sculptor at Blake. Zack Sengupta, who went to a prep school in the city but lived in our apartment building. A few others. I hadn't dated any of them for long, but I liked almost everything about the kissing.

There on Black Rock Beach, in the summer before my junior year, in the town that had been my home once before and now would be again, I discovered that I didn't know anything.

Kissing Jack was *nothing* like kissing any other boy I'd ever known. He put a hand against my neck, and his fingers were rough and warm, sending little earthquakes through my skin as they traced my ear and wound through my hair. His lips brushed against mine lightly at first, his lips barely parted. I heard myself make a sound, a faint moan, and Jack kissed me harder.

He twisted my hair between his fingers, kissing me along my chin and my jaw. I looked up to the moon and wondered what I was doing. After a few seconds, I gave up and let him hold me closer. But as I touched the soft worn fabric of his shirt, I involuntarily sucked in my breath. The electric response was immediate, the swirling, splintering flashes of a vision causing me to stumble. I tried to push him away before it went too far, before the visions claimed me, and I was thinking, *Not him, not him, please please just not him.*

But Jack pulled me back against him. He wrapped his strong arms around me and didn't say a word, and even through the skittering, flashing memories in my mind, the memories that weren't mine, the ones I didn't want to know, I was not able to resist. The attraction was too powerful, and I knew that if Jack released me I might fall, so I let the vision come while his chin bristled against my throat and made me tremble all the more.

Some sort of wall was lurching past, yelling, the sound of things breaking. No, wait, the wall was still, and I was running. I felt strong, I could run all night. Yes. Night. A parking lot, a brick building, pools of yellow light from tall streetlamps. Shouting. In my hand something heavy, something that felt right, all my anger coursing through my arm and into the thing I held as I smashed it against a window. The glass breaking, and for a moment I was—satisfied? No, not exactly, because the rage came back stronger. I needed to break something else, and fast, because my fury was like an itch in my skin, a burn in my veins, a scream lodged in my throat.

If I could just destroy something. If I could just destroy enough . . . Then maybe it would back down. Even a little. In my hands, the bat—yes, it was a baseball bat—landed hard and shattered another window.

And then the silvery veil floated down and I felt nothing but relief to be back in my own head, my own thoughts, my own memories.

I pushed my hands against Jack's chest, and this time he let me go. Stepping back, I wrapped my arms around myself. Now I *was* cold, misty spray from the gentle waves dampening my legs, the hem of my shorts.

Jack had done something terrible. I wasn't naïve—when you had a gift like mine, naïveté was a luxury you didn't get to keep. I'd seen all kinds of private deeds, enough that I understood that wrongdoing isn't limited to one kind of person, one fraction of society. Over the years I'd touched hundreds of articles of clothing. Trust me, you do too, you just don't realize it; people brush past you in crowds, buses, stores, school hallways, church. Unless you lock yourself in a room, you can't avoid it.

Teachers, camp counselors, businessmen, waitresses, priests, old people, and kids—there is no specific type of person, no particular occupation that signals secret wrongdoing, so I've never learned who to avoid.

I just really didn't want it to be Jack.

"What?" he asked roughly, no trace of warmth in his voice.

"I'm fine," I said quickly. "Just a little cold. Let's get back to the fire."

I started walking before he could reply, taking long strides and kicking up sand.

I was conscious of him following close behind. I *wanted* him to follow me. I didn't truly want to get away from him, only to try to understand what I had seen. Yes, it was violent and yes, I'd felt incredible anger. Jack was dangerous.

But I wanted to know more. And I couldn't forget the way his arms felt around me, the taste of his lips on mine.

· · ·

By the time we got back to the fire, Jack was walking apart from me, his hands jammed in his pockets. At the last minute I paused, close enough to see the glow of the fire reflected off his face, but far enough away that I could hear the laughter from the kids gathered around it, if not their words. I searched Jack's expression for signs of the turmoil that had marked the vision, but all I saw was frustration . . . and desire. I knew, because I felt it too, a heat that seared my insides even while my skin was chilled by the night air.

"I want to see you again," Jack muttered.

You do? I kept my expression as neutral as I could. Even after what I'd sensed, what I'd seen, I didn't want him any less. Looking into his eyes, into the darkness and the secrets, I sensed there was a lot more to him than he was letting on, that for every thought he shared, there were a dozen more that he didn't.

And . . . I wasn't afraid of him. Despite the powerful rage I'd sensed in his memories, I didn't believe it could ever be directed at me. But was that wishful thinking? Could he truly be dangerous?

I wanted to know more about him. I wanted to go deeper.

I wanted him to want me, and I couldn't resist his invitation. Maybe that was crazy, but when Jack grabbed my hand and pulled me against him, I hesitated before breaking away, and even then I only did it so I wouldn't have to endure the vision again.

"Do you have to work at your uncle's place during the week?"

"Yeah. Early. It opens at eight." He looked away, toward

the black ocean. "He's been sick. Lung cancer. He was lucky, they caught it in stage one."

"I'm sorry."

"He'll get better. What about you? What do you do during the week?"

"I work on my designs. I go out to thrift stores and garage sales and estate sales, and I scavenge vintage stuff." I knew I was rambling, and couldn't stop. "Clothes, fabric, buttons . . . everything, really. Then I take things apart and restyle them."

"Tomorrow's Sunday," Jack said, finally looking at me again. "They have garage sales on Sunday, right?"

"Uh, yes . . ."

"I'll drive."

I blinked. If I wasn't mistaken, Jack had just asked me out. Sort of. "Um, sure, yeah. Only, when I say scavenging . . . I'm talking one step up from Dumpster diving sometimes. I get stuff off curbs all the time."

"I don't have a problem with that. Maybe I'll learn something. What time?"

Tell him you're busy. I heard Rachel's voice in my head, coaching me on how to get a guy interested and keep him that way—and her system involved a *lot* of acting like you weren't really into him.

Which, now that I was talking to Jack, seemed sort of stupid. Even if it worked wonders for her—Rachel had seemingly never *not* gotten what she wanted.

"I'm sort of . . . flexible."

There was a burst of laughter from the other side of the campfire. I glanced over and saw that the horsing around had pretty much given way to more serious pursuits—drinking and talking, with a few kids making out or lying in the sand, wasted enough to simply stare at the moon.

Self-conscious, I backed away from Jack. I wasn't embarrassed to be seen with him. I just wasn't ready for everyone—especially Rachel—to know about it yet. I wanted it to be just . . . my secret, for a while.

"I'll pick you up at seven-thirty," Jack said. Not asking.

"You want the address?"

"I know where you live. The haunted dress shop."

CHAPTER NINE

I SAT ON THE CURB AT THE TOP of the hill with Giselle and Victoria, who were full-on drunk, wishing Rachel would hurry up. I just wanted to drive everyone home so I could get some sleep before Jack picked me up in the morning.

"So," Victoria said, yawning. "What's with you and Jack?"

"It's no big deal, we were just talking," I said, unsure how to navigate the conversation. "He was telling me about his dad."

"That was so sad," Giselle said. "When he died. Almost everyone at school went. We didn't even get into the main part of the church—we had to watch it on the big-screen TVs in the youth room. They had bagpipes. And firemen from practically the whole state."

"What about . . . after? I mean, Jack told me he went through a bad time for a while." For all I knew, everyone in town already knew about the drinking and drugs, but if not, they weren't going to hear it from me. But if there was more to it, maybe I could find out now.

Giselle frowned. "He told you about him and Amanda?" she asked coldly.

"Amanda who?"

"Amanda *Stavros*?"

The girl who disappeared. Whose name had been in the news for weeks. Her parents' frantic pleas broadcast on the news every night. "What about her?"

"Oh, you probably don't remember her from when you lived here," Giselle said. "She went to some private school down the coast until middle school."

"She was a sophomore, like us," Victoria said. "She was going out with Jack when she disappeared. The police talked to him after. He was one of the last people to see her."

"Talked to . . . as in, he was a suspect?"

"Yeah. I mean, it wasn't in the paper or whatever. I don't think they can do that, with minors, and he wasn't eighteen yet last year."

"You don't think he did it." I didn't mean for my words to come out as forcefully as they did, and Giselle glanced at me sharply.

"Well, the cops gave up on him, so I guess he didn't." She didn't bother to mask her sarcasm. "I mean, yeah, it's not like I think he killed her and dumped her body. But he sure didn't make things any easier for himself. He went nuts, Clare. If someone accused me of something that serious, I think I'd try to keep my shit together until they cleared me."

"Instead of . . ."

"Instead of everything. Vandalism, fights, drugs . . . He was locked up for a while, before his mom got a lawyer."

"You shouldn't tell her that, Giselle," Victoria said, slurring her words. "Clare can make up her own mind. If she likes him or not."

"But—he'd lost his dad," I protested. "And . . . and his girlfriend. I mean, he must have—" I thought of something else: Why hadn't Rachel told me any of this before? Why hadn't she said anything when I first met him?

"Look, I realize he's had a hard time," Giselle interrupted, her voice softening. "I feel sorry for him. But I'm just trying to protect you. Trust me, you don't want to get involved with him. This is a big year for you, you know?"

"Your mom would probably have a fit," Victoria added. "She's a hippie or something, right?"

"*My* mom?" I asked incredulously. Everyone had wildly inaccurate notions about our family, all because of Nana and things that had happened long ago. "Hardly. She's more the corporate type."

"Well, I still wouldn't want her to find out I was seeing him. If I were you."

"Why doesn't Rachel like him?" I asked, taking a chance.

"Oh, I don't think she hates him or anything, she's just really stressed about the Gold Key elections."

"What do you mean?"

"Elections are the first week of school. She's running for president, so she has to keep her reputation squeaky clean. I mean, it's ridiculous, but with Jack's suspension and his trouble with the police and all, she can't afford to be associated with him."

"But lots of people have been suspended," I said, wondering why Rachel had never mentioned she was running for president. "I mean, Luke has, twice, right?"

"That's different," Victoria said. "Luke's a Herrera. His dad owns, like, half of Monterey County."

"So?" I'd heard that Luke's dad was a wealthy real estate developer, but that wasn't exactly huge news in Winston. Many of the residents of the town were like us, middle-class families. But in the last few decades the hills above town had become prime real estate, and a lot of wealthy people moved down from Silicon Valley and San Francisco. Millionaires were a dime a dozen.

"So, if your dad gives a ton of money to the town, then you get away with anything. Come on, Clare, you're from the big city, I can't believe you're that naïve."

"My old school wasn't—" I didn't finish the sentence; there were plenty of rich kids at Blake too, but there was a sort of reverse elitism there. You were supposed to pretend you didn't care about money and status, that all that mattered was your art.

"Jack's family's poor," Giselle said, with the careful enunciation drunk people used when they were trying to make an obvious point. "Gold Key pretends they don't care about that, but they do. Just look at the membership list sometime."

"But if that's what they care about, I mean . . . Rachel's family is rich," I said.

"That's not the problem. Rachel only got in her sopho-more year, which never happens, and that's like a black mark against her. The alum advisory committee didn't even want to let her run, but they were the ones who made the exception for her in the first place."

"Can we stop talking about this?" Victoria said. "Clare and I aren't in your Diamond Butthole society, so this con-versation isn't doing much for me."

"Stop being so jealous," Giselle said, but she was laugh-ing. "It's not like anyone cares outside of this stupid town."

"Wait, what happened with Rachel?" I asked, confused.

"She didn't tell you?" Victoria looked surprised. "I thought you guys were like best friends."

"It was this huge scandal when she didn't get in fresh-man year," Giselle said. "Everyone thought she was in for sure, being a legacy and all, but she partied a lot in middle school."

"She did?" This was news to me. Rachel hid her party-ing incredibly well. To outside appearances, she was a model citizen.

Giselle and Victoria exchanged glances. "Yeah. Like, she got caught in the middle school bathroom getting high—"

"Her mom *lost* it," Victoria said. "She was grounded for like the whole summer; she and her mom fought for months. She snuck out a lot and—"

"Clare doesn't need to know about all *that*," Giselle said. Suddenly she didn't seem quite as drunk as before, and I got an eerie sense that maybe Gold Key membership really did mean something to these girls. Come to think of it, the girls who were members partied with the rest of the crowd, but they stopped short of anything that would look bad, anything that would reflect poorly on them or each other. "All you need to know is that Rachel worked really, really hard freshman year to restore her reputation. And when Amanda disappeared, they had a spot to fill, and they picked Rachel."

"And now she's running for president."

"Were you guys, like, really close to Amanda?" I asked.

Both of them shrugged, and they exchanged a glance. "Not really. I mean, I don't know if anyone was. Everyone liked her and all, but . . . it was like she didn't have *best* friends, just more like . . . casual friends."

"She was into guys," Giselle said. "More than other girls. Y'know?"

I figured I did. I'd known girls like that, who went from guy to guy without ever taking a break in between, who kept other girls at a distance.

"Okay," Victoria interrupted. "New subject. Are you guys going to Dillon's memorial tomorrow?"

"Yeah, everyone is," Giselle said. "You should come with us, Clare."

Yet another thing Rachel hadn't mentioned. Maybe she didn't know about it either, though that seemed unlikely. I was starting to get really confused about my relationship with her—it seemed like there was a lot she hadn't told me. "Um, I guess I could, depending on when it is. Are they having one for Amanda too?"

"No, her mom's not into it, I guess. It's Dillon's parents

who planned this whole service. They put a lot of effort into it."

"It's at two down at Raley Park," Giselle said. I wondered if they knew the park was named after the same family my crazy grandmother had married into, the family whose mansion she now lived in. "It's not going to last long. I can pick you up if you want. Then you can come over after. My folks are making me stay in, because of the ax murderer."

That got them giggling, which made me feel queasy. It was weird how none of the kids seemed to take the anniversary very seriously, but maybe it was some sort of post-traumatic stress thing, a way to compartmentalize the fear and horror of losing someone they'd all known.

"Mrs. Granger stopped by today to talk to my mom about the house walk," I said. "She was really nice."

"She's amazing," Giselle said. "I mean, after what happened? She says it helps her heal to give back to the town. But Mr. Granger's another story."

"He's, like, insane," Victoria said. "Did you ever see him at a game?"

"He got in a lot of trouble a few years ago," Giselle explained for my benefit. "He got in a fight with another father at one of Dillon's baseball games."

"The refs threw him out. He was always yelling at them from the stands. He yelled at Dillon too. He ended up getting barred from the games and practices. He was going to sue for a while, but I guess Mrs. Granger talked him out of it."

"He's not like that since they lost Dillon," Giselle said. "I mean, you see him around town but he hardly even talks anymore."

"Yeah, but he *stares* at you. At all the kids. Haven't you noticed? They go to my church." Victoria shivered. "My mom won't sit anywhere near him."

"I can't imagine losing a child," I said, feeling a ridiculous urge to defend someone I'd never met.

"Yeah, I guess it could mess you up. Mrs. Stavros is a drunk now. And Amanda's dad took off a few months after she disappeared. Couldn't handle it."

"She used to be so beautiful," Giselle sighed. "Did you know she was a model?"

"It's true," Victoria confirmed. "She did ads, maybe? Catalogs? Amanda's dad was a *lot* older. I think he went back to Greece or something."

Rachel popped up along the path at that moment, out of breath. "I got to pee so bad," she announced.

"Well, do it before you get in the car," I said. "Since I borrowed my mom's."

Mom was still reluctant to let me take the car, since I'd barely passed my license test. I didn't get a lot of practice until she bought a car when we found out we were moving back to Winston. I talked her into loaning it to me by reminding her that I needed practice, and swearing that I wouldn't have anything to drink.

And by reminding her that most of the girls I was driving were Gold Key members, which usually served to make people imagine halos over their heads.

We dropped Victoria off first, drove up into the hills where the rich people lived and dropped off Giselle, and then it was only me and Rachel. I drove to her house and parked in the driveway. She was drunker than I'd realized, and she swayed back and forth in the front seat.

"Hey, don't throw up in here, okay?" I asked anxiously.

Rachel giggled. I knew I should wait until she was sober to talk to her, but I couldn't help it. "Why didn't you tell me about Jack?" I demanded, with more irritation than I intended.

"What about him?"

"About him and Amanda Stavros? That they were dating? That he was a suspect in her disappearance?"

"Oh, Cee-Cee . . ." She hiccupped. "That's . . . that's."

"How about the fact that he was arrested? Think you could have mentioned that? I had to hear about it from Giselle and Victoria!"

"I woulda told you," she said, slurring her words, "if you'd started dating him or something. I wouldn't have let that happen."

"*Let* it happen? What about letting me make my own decisions? What about telling me what you know about him so I could decide?"

"What're you so mad about? I was trying to protect you."

That made me even angrier, but I wasn't sure why. After all, I believed her—Rachel probably thought she was doing the right thing. "You don't think I can handle myself with a guy like him, is that it?"

Her head lolled toward me and she looked at me with

wide eyes. "He was never cleared, you know. Some people still think he did it. That he killed Amanda."

"Well, great. So you didn't warn me that he was a *murderer*?" I knew that part of my frustration was directed at myself, at how attracted I was to Jack, even knowing what I knew about him. It would have been way easier if I could like an honors student, or at least Kane De Ponceau, who wasn't guilty of anything except getting drunk and stupid, as far as I could tell.

"Cee-Cee . . . Okay, forget it. Jack didn't kill her."

"How do you know?"

To my surprise, her eyes welled with tears and she snuffled against the sleeve of the sweatshirt she'd borrowed. "He just . . . didn't. There were other people involved."

"Other people involved in what?"

"Everything," she said vaguely, waving her hands, hitting one of them against the passenger window. "Ow. Dillon and Amanda and everything."

"Are you saying you know something about who killed them?"

"It's just . . . Oh, never mind, I shouldn't have said anything, okay? Jack thinks he's better than everyone else because he doesn't party. But if you want to go out with him then I guess you can."

I could tell I was losing her attention; her eyelids were sliding down and she looked like she was about to fall asleep. "Do you know something?" I asked again, with more urgency. Rachel had never talked to me like this when she was sober. I put my hand on her arm and shook it gently.

Then, as an afterthought, I touched the hem of the shirt she was wearing under the sweatshirt, the one she'd changed into after she took off the beach dress, but the clothes had nothing to tell me. Which wasn't surprising: Rachel and her mom were huge shoppers, and her shirt was new.

"Mrs. Stavros does."

"Does what?"

"She knows. She has . . ."

Rachel made a face and hiccupped gently, and then she got the car door open just in time to throw up on her parents' driveway.

• • •

After getting Rachel up to her room, I drove home, preoccupied with Dillon Granger and Amanda Stavros. I was thinking back to a year ago. Mom had taken off all four days of the holiday weekend, which was practically unheard of, and we got to go out on a boat belonging to her ex-boss. We went to a concert in Golden Gate park, and shopping downtown. It had been a good weekend.

And three hours away, in the town I grew up in, a girl my age had been taken, most likely murdered.

In my room, my laptop's screen saver flashed pictures from the last Blake School exhibit I'd taken part in. There were Lincoln's copper tubing sculptures, weird landscapes in oil pastel by my friend Maura. Caleb's photos, which I never had the heart to tell him looked like the ones I had taken on my mom's phone when I was in grade school. And my masterpiece from last year: a sixties cherry red wool swing coat I'd taken apart and painstakingly reconstructed, tailoring it perfectly for myself, lining it with camel-colored silk. Lincoln had gone with me to a notion shop in Oakland to buy the buttons, which were made of genuine bone. Even impossible-to-please Mrs. Bertrand had grudgingly admired the finished product, and gave me an A for the semester; too bad it would hardly ever get cold enough to wear it in Winston.

I really needed to call the rest of my old friends. Lincoln and I had talked about all of them visiting in August, and he said he'd ask to borrow his dad's Lexus and bring Maura and Caleb with him.

I was happier about moving than I'd expected to be. I had NewToYou and Rachel and now Jack, but I missed things about my old life, too. I missed our taco truck lunches on the steps of the school, the vegan kids glaring at us as we licked our greasy fingers. I missed trips to Buffalo Exchange, the best vintage clothing store ever. I missed nights up on Lincoln's roof deck talking about the boys we liked.

But I wasn't ready for my old world and my new friends to collide. Not quite yet, not until I figured out the situation with Jack, not until things were more settled. I promised myself I'd call everyone later in the week.

I watched the screen saver for a few minutes, letting it cycle through the images twice. Then I took a deep breath and Googled Jack. I knew that any official police reports wouldn't be public, since he had been a minor when he got into trouble, but you never knew what would turn up online.

I scrolled through the hits. There were a few articles about Amanda, in which Jack was listed as a friend, nothing more. There were no reports of his arrest or suspension. I found a few mentions of him in articles from sources as far away as Monterey about the soccer team, and it appeared that he really had been a good player.

I wasn't finding anything to help put my mind at ease, and it felt a bit wrong to be looking. Okay, a lot wrong, even if Jack was practically a stranger. He didn't know about my weird gift, about the visions. Wasn't it wrong to go around behind his back? To spy on him?

Except he hadn't told me much about himself. He could be trouble—big trouble, if he hadn't really reformed the way he implied. Rachel said he was innocent, and even if she wouldn't tell me why, my intuition agreed—at least, I thought Jack was innocent of hurting Amanda. But wouldn't it be stupid to make that assumption without any proof?

Unable to decide one way or another, I typed in Amanda's name instead. Maybe something would turn up there, a quote or interview or something. I wanted to know more, especially since Jack had dated her. I was curious, and there was something else, some uneasy, scared feeling that was nagging in the back of my mind.

I hit "Enter."

There were over a thousand results. I clicked on "Images," and my screen was tiled with pictures of her, a beautiful young girl in a cheerleading outfit, in a photo with her parents, in her official school picture—

I froze, unable to breathe.

There, over and over, sprinkled among the other images, was a photo of a laughing dark-haired girl in front of a bush blooming with pink flowers, wearing the denim jacket that was stuffed in a box in my closet. The one that had knocked me out, that practically buzzed with terrifying energy, had belonged to a girl who disappeared.

I knew it had to be the same jacket because of the unmistakable details: the distinctive topstitching, the twisted placket that was a hallmark of Ripley Couture sportswear, the crested silver buttons, the striped silk lining. And I'd lay odds that Amanda was a size small, judging from her fine bone structure and lean figure. What were the chances of two of the same expensive designer jacket showing up in a tiny town like Winston? It was practically impossible.

I scanned several of the articles, but learned nothing new. I'd seen it all on the news over the past year. Still, there was something nagging at the back of my mind. . . .

A memory popped into my head, the borrowed memory from Lara's vision. The long-haired girl who'd been at Dell Market . . . It hadn't clicked before, but I suddenly realized what had been nagging at my mind: she had been wearing the jacket. It had been *Amanda,* getting ready to party with the crowd I now was trying so hard to belong to. All I could see in the vision was her profile, but it was the same girl on my screen, wearing the same jacket. The distance between me and this stranger, this girl who'd disappeared a year ago, was starting to close. I couldn't pretend much longer that I didn't care about what happened to her.

Rachel knew things she wasn't telling me. All of it seemed connected, and not in a good way. The people I knew best, the people I cared about in Winston, had a dark side that I had only begun to recognize, much less understand.

But somehow I was being pulled right into the middle of it all. The jacket in the box was Amanda's, I was sure of it. But how had it gotten filthy and torn? How did it end up in a plastic bag on a junk dealer's table?

And what was I supposed to do with it now?

• • •

When you can't sleep, you turn to your tried and true methods for dealing with insomnia, right? But the harder you try, the more you toss and turn. Lincoln used to get crazed around test time—he wasn't a good test taker—and he told me he would count backward from one hundred, imagining each number scrawled on a sketch pad. My mom had a secret stash of sleeping pills that she would take in a pinch, never more than once or twice a month.

Me? I got out my ripper.

A seam ripper is a little plastic-handled sewing tool about the size of a ballpoint pen. At one end is a sharp metal point with a fishhook-shaped blade. You poke the point behind a stitch in a seam in a piece of clothing that you want to un-sew. Carefully, because you don't want to cut the fabric itself, you hook the stitch on the point and slide it down the curved-blade part, which cuts the thread. Now you have two tiny thread ends poking out of the seam of the garment.

So far so good. But the really satisfying part comes next. You use the sharp point to tease out the threads, undoing a few more stitches until you have a big enough hole in the seam that you can hook your fingers in. Which you do—and then you pull.

Rrrrrrip!

There's a kind of muffled popping sound as the fabric comes apart. You can't pull too hard or you can damage the garment, and you can only pull out a few inches of stitching before you have to start over again by cutting the threads, but it's incredibly relaxing, undoing in seconds something that took ages to create, knowing that you'll put it back together again and make something entirely new.

I dragged my big tub of vintage finds from the sewing room and rooted around in it until I found the perfect piece to work on, a pair of thin-wale corduroy pants, low-waisted and narrow-legged, in a pale green. Size 8—my size. I'd already tried them on and they fit perfectly through the waist and hips.

It was just the leg I didn't like. I didn't have a problem with skinny jeans, but I thought it was a look that was best left to denim, dark denim with a bit of Lycra for stretch. These pants were crying out to be something different.

I'd gotten my inspiration from an old magazine article I found online about Veruschka, who was a German model in the sixties. In one picture she was wearing a pair of jeans with a triangular patch set in from hem to knee that turned ordinary trousers into bell bottoms. In the photo I had printed and tacked to the wall above my sewing table, the designer had used a bright orange paisley fabric, not even bothering to hide the fact that the inset was an after-thought. That was what I intended for the green pants, and I had the perfect fabric set aside to enhance them—a washable home-furnishing-weight linen printed with a wild floral design in black and russet.

But tonight all that mattered was that the inseam had to be ripped, hem to knee.

I played some old Joan Baez to get in the mood, and bent over my task with my bright OttLite focused on the tiny stitches. They disappeared into the velourlike wale of the corduroy, and it took me a while to find the perfect one to start with. I poked the ripper's point underneath and slit the stitch, teasing a few more out on either side, carefully unraveling the hem so that I could separate the leg panels, and then—when I had a firm grasp on the pieces—I gave a mighty tug.

Rrrrrrip.

The seam gave way with a satisfying sound, cotton thread popping and the fabric separating easily. Later this week, I would carefully pin the gusset in place, using a dozen pins on either side, making sure it was eased in perfectly so that the pant leg hung correctly.

When I had the seams separated the way I wanted, I folded the pants in thirds and laid them out on my ironing board, ready for tomorrow. Then I turned out the light and made the short trip to my bedroom, where I got under the cool cotton sheets and glanced at my alarm clock.

One-thirty. And Jack was picking me up at seven-thirty. Okay. Leaving an hour for a shower, a speed blow-dry, and a little makeup, I'd still get enough sleep to keep a normal human fueled for a day. Enough, maybe, to dispel the sense that I was going crazy.

I switched off my iPod, but not before hearing Joan rasp her way through "Scarlet Ribbons."

Through the night my heart was aching
Just before the dawn was breaking . . .

I'd always loved that song, but I'd never really listened to the lyrics until now, and suddenly I understood that it wasn't a lullaby at all, but something much darker. A mother overhears her child praying for ribbons in her hair, and in the morning, finds red ribbons tangled on the girl's pillow. But who left them, and why? Listening to the haunting melody, I felt certain that the visitor invaded the locked house with evil on his mind. Long after I drifted off, the music continued playing in the background of my dreamless sleep.

CHAPTER TEN

I was waiting for Jack on the porch by seven-fifteen, the morning fog drifting in from the ocean. Steam lifted from the two mugs of strong coffee I'd brewed. For me, caffeine was a necessity—I hadn't slept that well, tossing and turning until the sky finally lightened with the approach of dawn.

I'd borrowed my mom's concealer to try to cover the dark circles under my eyes, and chose what was, for me anyway, a pretty tame outfit: long embroidered Indian-cotton skirt that flared around my ankles, a T-shirt from a San Francisco club band that Lincoln liked, and a thick black belt I'd found in the men's department of the Valencia Street Salvation Army. I'd had to cut off almost a foot of the length to make it fit, piercing the leather with a punch needle and blanket-stitching it with waxed thread to finish the raw edges, but it was worth the effort for the buckle alone, hammered silver in the shape of Texas with a turquoise cabochon inset for the capitol. I topped it all off with a zipped gray Blake School sweatshirt that was literally falling apart at the seams. The sweatshirt had been Lincoln's when he was a freshman, and when he outgrew it the following year he gave it to me. It reminded me of him, our close relationship, so I had never bothered to fix it.

I had never had a sibling—well, my dad's new wife had a baby the winter before, a little boy named Caesar, but I still hadn't met him—and Lincoln was the closest thing I had to a brother. Years earlier, before my parents split, I'd hoped for a brother. Dad never paid much attention to me, and somehow in my five-year-old brain, I had decided it was because I was a girl. Nana was happy to play dolls and fairies and princesses with me, and I figured that if I had a brother, Dad would play with him—boy things, baseball and trucks and firemen—and I could join in.

I should have realized that the problem wasn't ever me. Dad was just selfish, the kind of guy who couldn't tear himself away from the sports page or the Internet long enough to spend a few minutes with his kid. The kind of guy who'd throw everything away for a fling with his young, sexy assistant. Now that Dad did have a son of his own, I wondered if the new baby was getting much attention. Somehow I doubted it.

I heard Jack's car before I saw it, the sound of the engine not exactly purring. I don't know what I had been expecting, but it sure wasn't the ancient Datsun pickup that shuddered to a stop in front of my house. It had once been white, but there were rusted areas that had been sanded and primed, and a couple of panels that had been replaced, one red, one brown, giving it a patchwork effect.

Jack came around the car wearing sunglasses that masked any expression on his face. In a single night I'd convinced myself he was the boy of my dreams, then started wondering if he was violent and unstable, and how he fit into the story of the horror hidden in my closet. I wished I'd never touched the jacket, never Googled Amanda's name, but now I knew I had to find out more. I wouldn't rest until I understood what had happened to Amanda and, quite possibly, Dillon.

Jack took the stairs two at a time. Our porch looked out over the water, with another row of houses one street below, and then the Beach Road, but I thought our views were better—and we could never have afforded the closer street anyway. The only reason we could live this close to the water at all was that the house had been in the family, all the way back to my great-grandmother.

Which in a way kind of made up for being branded as the freak family in the haunted house. No matter what anyone else thought, I had been a part of this town from even before my birth. My great-great-grandmother Alma's legacy lived on through me, not just through my sewing, but through the gift I carried in my blood. I might not have ever asked for the visions, but they bound me to Winston in ways that only Nana could ever really understand.

"Hey, Clare."

I offered Jack the coffee cup as he sat in the other wicker

chair. Mom had found the chairs when we'd gone scavenging at a farm sale, and painted them a creamy color that complemented the sage green of the house. I'd been meaning to make chair cushions for her as a surprise, but the truth was, it was so much more fun to work on clothes that I never got around to the home décor projects Mom wanted done—curtains for the kitchen, a fabric panel to hide the pipes below the sink in the guest bathroom.

"Do you want cream or sugar?" I asked, feeling awkwardly formal.

"No. Thanks."

In the steely light of morning, his eyes were a clear gray, like the ocean itself. Caleb had told me that gray mornings provided some of the best light for portrait photography—now I saw why.

"Listen, Jack . . . There's something I wanted to ask you about. But maybe not here. My mom sleeps late on the weekends, but . . ."

"We can talk on the way," Jack said. "Where's our first stop?"

I told him about the garage sale I'd found on Craigslist, north and a few miles inland, in the town of Palacios. It was home to ranchers and people escaping the city, and the seasonal population swelled with farmhands and migrant workers. Sometimes these inland raids yielded great vintage finds—boxes of old clothes that had been abandoned in attics and sheds and garages, things most people wouldn't give a second look. Many were unusable, but occasionally I'd find woolens or silks that could be used to add interesting touches to more modern garments. If nothing else, I raided them for buttons. A patch here, a closure there; these were the details that made my designs unique.

The ride was beautiful. The fog dissipated as soon as we left the town limits, and we drove along a two-lane road winding through gentle hills and fields of berries and lettuce, corn, and tomatoes.

Jack's driving surprised me. He was a careful driver, never pushing the old truck over the speed limit. It smelled nice, a combination of motor oil, sunbaked vinyl, and tobacco, among other things I couldn't name.

"Dad and I were going to restore this truck together," Jack said abruptly. "He was still teaching me how to do the bodywork when he died."

I didn't know what to say, so instead I cautiously changed the subject. "Look, Jack . . . about what I wanted to ask you."

"Yeah?"

I was silent for a moment, trying to decide where to start. I couldn't very well bring up my vision—the baseball bat, the broken windows—unless I could explain how I knew about them. And I had no way to do that without lying. But maybe I could work around to the subject another way.

"It's about Amanda Stavros."

The change in him was instant. His facial features went from taut to angry, and his hands gripped the wheel tightly. Still, when he spoke, his voice was calm and unemotional.

"What do you want to know?"

"I . . . heard you used to date her."

"Yeah, I did, off and on. It was no big thing, despite . . . whatever you've heard."

"I—I haven't heard anything," I said, surprised.

He raised his eyebrows behind his mirrored sunglasses. "No?" he asked softly, a deadly edge to his voice. "And yet, here you are asking me about it."

His bitterness stung, and there was something else—a faint tendril of fear, of wondering whether I had misjudged him. Clearly, he had more of a temper than I had realized. But enough to escalate to rage? To violence? "I'm just, I thought that since you knew her—"

"Along with a thousand other people. Amanda wasn't exactly shy, Clare. And there were guys she dated besides me. We weren't exactly exclusive."

"But no one—"

"You want to know about that time, I'll tell you. But I have to warn you, I don't have a lot to say, especially considering it messed up my life for a while. Not my relationship with Amanda—that part of it was no big deal."

"You weren't serious with her?"

"No."

He answered quickly—too quickly. Not the way I would have expected from someone whose girlfriend had disappeared. So maybe they weren't in love, but still, Amanda must have meant *something* to Jack. I couldn't imagine losing even a casual friend to something like what had happened—but Jack was behaving as though her loss didn't matter to him at all.

"How did you end up dating her, anyway?" I asked him.

Jack took a deep breath, slowly exhaling as he kept his eyes on the road. "Amanda was in my English class. At first I noticed her for the same reason everyone else did—I mean, you've seen what she looked like. But she and I were assigned to do a report on *Fahrenheit 451* together. I had a hard time getting through that book, but Amanda loved it. She came over to my house a lot. I think she didn't want to be at home. At first it was cool, because we talked about books and . . . things. But she was different in school."

"Different how?"

"She liked the attention. Girls, guys, teachers, it didn't matter. She acted stupid at school, and when I called her out on it, she got really . . ."

His voice trailed off and his skin flushed. "Aggressive," he finally said. "Sexually. After we argued, she always wanted—it was almost like she liked it better if we were . . . fighting. I wasn't into that, which is one of the reasons we kind of grew apart."

Now I was the one who blushed. Not because I had trouble understanding what he was telling me, but because I'd imagined what he would be like. What it would be like to be with him. Now I wondered if I was crazy, to be attracted to someone so volatile.

"So when she disappeared, you're saying other people blamed you?" I said, trying to refocus the conversation.

"Not at first. There was all that serial killer speculation in the news. But it was only a day or two before the cops showed up at my house. And yeah, Detective Kostelic—he was the one who got to play bad cop—he had it in for me.

Kept it up for weeks. Told me if he had his way my record would never be sealed, it would follow me around so every woman I ever met would know I was a killer. Oh, and my mom—she *says* she doesn't blame me for Dad's accident, but since it happened the day after I was taken in for questioning, the timing was kind of bad, you know what I mean?"

"So they accused you of murder." I acted like I was learning this for the first time, but given what he'd told me about him and Amanda, it wouldn't have come as a surprise. If I'd been one of the cops on the case, I would have suspected Jack too, especially if he'd allowed his temper to get the better of him when they questioned him.

"Not outright, other than Detective Kostelic a couple of times when there was no one else in the room." Jack laughed bitterly. "There were a *lot* of implications. They kept coming around to talk, upsetting my mom. After a couple months they finally arrested me for vandalism and possession. It was almost a relief, just to have them *do* something."

Like in my vision. I remembered the feeling of rage, the borrowed emotion that made my own fingers twitch with the longing to break things, to lash out. Jack's anger was real. His quiet exterior did not mask the simmering fury on the inside. I had to figure out if it was controlled, or dangerous, before I got any closer to him.

"I'm sorry for what your mom went through," I said stiffly. I was sincere about that, at least.

"Yeah. She worked with the lawyer Dad hired. She

made sure he stayed on it. He did most of my talking for me. I had less than an ounce of pot, so they tried to get me on a felony charge of intent to sell, but the judge had to throw all the charges out."

"What about the vandalism?"

Jack shrugged. "I was drunk and I wrecked a section of the fence at the high school with some kids. We spray-painted a shed and broke some windows."

Of course, that was only what he'd been *caught* doing. There was always the possibility that he'd done more than that, maybe a lot more, and not been caught.

Jack had been driving faster as he talked, taking the dips and turns in the rural roads at a speed that spun gravel and made the tires complain against the pavement.

"Hey, are you trying to kill us both?" I demanded, then realized how the question sounded and clamped my mouth shut. But Jack put on the brakes and concentrated on the road, his jaw tight.

For a few minutes we rode in silence, and I thought about what Rachel had said. *I was trying to protect you.* And then, only a moment later, she had insisted that Jack didn't kill Amanda. What did she know? Did she think Jack might be capable of more violence? Of hurting me?

Was I crazy for taking a chance that he wouldn't?

"Listen, Jack, the thing is, something happened last night," I said, determined to figure out what he knew, what part he had played, if any. "After I got home."

Jack glanced at me warily. "When you left the beach?"

"Yes. It was late. There's something . . . I mean, you're

one of the only people I've met so far who actually knew Amanda. You know things about her that could, I don't know, help me understand."

Jack seemed, if anything, to grow even angrier. Up ahead was a boarded-up produce stand, the old and tired predecessor to a new one that had been constructed half a mile down the road at an intersection where drivers would be more likely to pull over. Jack coasted off the road, the truck jouncing over the shoulder onto the dirt parking lot and pulling up under the shade of a group of tall, leafy trees. A pair of wild turkeys squawked, scattering into the overgrown weeds behind the shed as Jack cut the engine.

He turned to me, his frown deepening, his eyes narrowed. "So all of this—last night, on the beach, coming out with me today—was this all a way for you to get close to me so you could ask about her?"

"What? *No!*" I couldn't believe he would think that. "I didn't even know who she was until yesterday. A few of us rode home together, they were talking . . ."

Jack said nothing for a while, just stared out at the ruined shack with his arms folded tightly across his chest, breathing shallowly. He was *furious,* and I felt a range of emotions I could barely keep track of. Regret, certainly—a part of me wished I'd never brought up her name. Suspicion—wondering what Amanda had really meant to him, and whether he'd had anything to do with what happened to her. And underneath it, that thread of attraction I couldn't ignore, even when I told myself this was a dangerous game to play.

Except it wasn't a game. Jack was willful and stubborn, moody, angry and passionate. And I was more than a little afraid of him. But last night, when he'd wrapped his arms around me as we stood in the ocean, the salt water caressing our feet, I hadn't been able to pull away. I'd wanted him despite the danger, and I wanted him now.

How much would it take to provoke him? He said Amanda had been too dramatic for him, but that was vague. Maybe it was something else. Had she done something to anger him? Had she led him on, then turned him down? Dumped him for another guy?

All those things were possible. All of them had the potential to enrage him. I had hoped that Jack could help me understand who Amanda had been, and somehow relieve me of any responsibility so I could get rid of the jacket and sever my connection to her. Instead, I felt like my attraction to him made that connection both deeper and more dangerous.

"Listen," he finally said, still not looking at me. "There've been . . . others."

"Other what?"

"Other girls . . . like you. Coming on to me, when what they really wanted was, I don't know. They had some sort of sick fascination with Amanda."

"I don't understand."

"No? You should talk to Maybeth Layne. You'll meet her when school starts. She's on some exchange program in Italy right now."

"What about her?"

"After I got arrested, she started acting really interested in me. I mean, I got used to that fast—there's always going to be girls who want trouble, who like guys their parents will hate. At first I thought that was what it was and I just kind of ignored her. But she kept it up. Asking me all these questions about what Amanda and I had done together.

"Finally I figured out that she thought I was guilty, that I really had done something to Amanda. And that she was going to figure it out, maybe be a hero. Maybe get the attention she wanted. I don't know, I guess she thought I'd confess to her if she was nice enough to me.

"For a while it got better. Then one weekend she asked me to help her study at her house, which I should have seen right through, because she didn't ever care about her grades—and in her room she had all these pictures. She had access to them from being on yearbook staff. Amanda on the cheer squad, Amanda with her friends at Kitty's Korner, Amanda in chem lab. She had them pinned up on her bulletin board. I asked her about it and she gave me this funny smile. 'I just thought maybe if you saw this you'd want to tell me what happened,' she said. And I told her I didn't know what she was talking about, and she said she thought we had a special connection."

He shook his head, as if trying to dislodge the memory. "Some special fucking connection. Her dad ended up calling Detective Kostelic and telling him I was harassing his daughter. So I got to go through it all again—cops at my house, getting hauled in, Mom calling the lawyer. All of it."

I didn't know what to say. I felt sick to my stomach—I couldn't imagine what that girl had been looking for, if it had been a game to her, satisfying her curiosity, or if she'd been interested in Jack all along.

I also had no proof that he was telling the truth. What if he'd made it all up? What if he really had been harassing Maybeth?

But he wasn't harassing me. He hadn't done anything that crossed any lines, yet. I tried to consider him objectively, but in the soft morning light that filtered into the truck, it was impossible not to notice the glints of red-gold in his black hair, the deep brown skin, the muscles tight in his neck, his arms, his broad shoulders. His eyes in this light were darker than they had been earlier, almost a cloudy gray-blue, and with his features tight with anger, the traces of his adolescent self were almost entirely gone. His was the face of a man, not a boy.

Of *course* girls would notice him. Of course they would want him. And the mystique around him, the trouble he'd been in, made him more attractive—at least to certain girls. So he questioned everyone's interest in him, wondering if it was genuine or merely a cover-up for sensationalism and attention-seeking.

"You don't have to believe me," I said. "But I'm just trying to understand."

Jack didn't look at me. He was staring straight out the windshield at the leaning shack, at the shelves that held a few empty berry baskets and a lot of cobwebs.

"When Dillon disappeared, it was really sad, but I didn't pay all that much attention," I tried to explain. "It had been a long time since I lived in Winston. I was busy. But then after Amanda disappeared, when they started saying it could be a serial killer, that her body might never be found, suddenly it was all over the news. It was like you couldn't get away from it. But it still wasn't real, you know? It wasn't until we moved back here and I started meeting kids who knew her. Then it started to affect me more."

"Why, Clare?" His voice was quiet but intense. "Why can't you just let it be? She's not coming back. It's been almost a year. People don't talk about her and Dillon anymore. The town . . . the town is finally starting to get over it. It's been months since Detective Kostelic has even driven by my house."

I wasn't about to tell him why it was different for me, about what I could do. I'd only told two other people about my gift, and it hadn't exactly gone well. My mother had forbidden me from ever mentioning it again. It had gone better with Nana; she'd helped me understand why I was the way I was, and made me feel less like a freak. And she'd told me I had a choice. But there was still so much I didn't understand, and with the jacket, I felt like I'd been given a task I couldn't refuse. To find out what had really happened to her and, maybe, to make it right.

I didn't think Amanda was alive. But someone had been responsible. Someone who was out there now, who had possibly killed a little boy, who maybe would do it again if he wasn't caught.

I could ask Jack to take me home. I could pretend we never talked about Amanda, pass him in the halls without speaking to him when school started, and he'd fade into the background where he evidently spent most of his time anyway. It was the smart thing to do, the least risky. I'd throw myself into life with Rachel's crowd, maybe walk on the beach with Luke next time—with any luck I'd have a boyfriend this fall. I could throw out the box of clothes, carry it down the hill to the Dumpster behind the Seagull Inn.

But as I stared at Jack's profile, in the pleasant warmth of the old truck, I knew that wasn't what was going to happen. The jacket had come to me because some . . . spirit, some *force*, wanted me to have it, to touch it, to find out what happened. Or at least that was what it felt like. And the choice did not feel like mine to make. Just as I had never asked for the gift in the first place, I had not asked to be drawn into a girl's disappearance, but something had been put into motion and I had a strong feeling I had to follow.

I wasn't going to walk away from Jack, even if it was the smart thing to do. I could trust him—or I could be careful, and trust myself to stay a step ahead.

And what I wanted, right now, despite all my suspicions and fears, was to touch him.

He said nothing as I slowly reached across the seat and

touched his sleeve, lightly at first, my fingertips brushing against the soft flannel. The shirt had been washed dozens of times; I could tell from the worn nap, the puckering along the seam where the thread had shrunk more than the fibers in the fabric.

I felt so many emotions when I touched Jack. Desire. Doubt. Suspicion.

But this shirt had no stories to tell.

CHAPTER ELEVEN

JACK SLAMMED HIS HAND OVER MINE, so fast I barely saw him move.

"Don't start this. Not unless you're serious."

I caught my breath, pulling my hand back, as though his touch burned me. And, in a way, it had; it ignited something inside me that I'd never felt around a boy before.

I knew if I'd left my hand where it was, things would have gone farther. Maybe a lot farther. And suddenly I wasn't sure I was ready.

"So there's one other thing," I said, acting like it hadn't happened. "I saw this picture of Amanda online, where she's wearing a Ripley Couture denim jacket. I bought the exact same jacket from a junk dealer the other day. It was pretty torn up and dirty but I am positive it's hers. Decorative stitching on the front, silver buttons—do you remember it?"

Jack regarded me skeptically. "I mean, yeah, she had a denim jacket she liked, but so does almost every other girl. How can you be sure it's the same one?"

"Jack, this is what I *do*," I said. "I know fashion, and that was a really expensive jacket that you can't get down here. You'd have to go to San Francisco or L.A. I was just wondering . . . was she wearing it the day she disappeared?"

Jack scowled at me for a moment. "You're not going to let this drop, are you."

"I just . . . can't."

He sighed. "That week, the weather was good. Not too hot during the day, no rain, but it got chilly at night. Amanda kept that jacket in her car, and she wore it over whatever she had on when she got cold.

"You know, when they took me in for questioning, they asked me what she was wearing that day. I couldn't tell them. I don't notice shit like that. I mean, she always looked nice, I guess. I'd seen her earlier in the day—we had lunch in town—and she wanted to get together that night but I couldn't. Mom had invited Arthur over for dinner. But Amanda didn't take no for an answer."

"Did you tell the police that?"

"Of course I did. The problem was, Arthur left early and my folks went to bed, so the cops said I could have left the house any time that night."

"But why did they think . . . you know, that you did it? I mean, just the fact that you were dating, that doesn't seem like enough."

Jack didn't answer me for a moment. His mood seemed to turn even darker as he stared out the window at nothing.

"She had texted me. A few times. Eight times, between

that afternoon and evening. The last one was around ten-thirty, so they said I went to meet her then. Her mom went to the police that night to report her missing, but it wasn't until the next morning that they came to our house. Dad was out on a job. They asked for my phone and I gave it to them. They asked to search our house, and Mom and I let them. Dad . . ."

His voice trailed off and he paused for a moment, anger gathering in his eyes again. "Dad called the lawyer, after they left. He didn't trust the cops. He'd had some bad experiences with them, a long time ago. But they had my phone."

"What were the text messages? Was it something that made them think you were, that you had had a fight or something?"

"Amanda . . . took pictures of herself. And the messages were explicit."

"Oh." My face went hot again. I had never sexted anyone, but there was a lot of it going on at Blake, where, of course, they had their own special way of doing things—when girls took pictures of themselves, they were likely to be artful shots with props. Lincoln thought it was hilarious; he loved to make me uncomfortable by forwarding me the pictures that went around. He said I was the last virgin at Blake, a fact I'd sworn him to keep secret forever.

Suddenly that seemed like such a long time ago.

"The police . . . they never come out and say exactly what they think," Jack muttered. "I mean, it was obvious they were trying to put a case together, but they never found enough evidence. Because there wasn't any. I didn't even text her back after the first time. All I said was I'd talk to her later. And I erased the messages. They got records from AT&T but they couldn't prove anything."

Yet another time when I had to choose whether to believe him. "Did the lawyer help?"

"He told my mom there was no case. The cops tried to make a thing about the fact that my dad called him right away, like that meant I was guilty or something. But they backed off pretty fast."

"I'm . . . sorry. For what you went through." And I was—if he was telling the truth.

"You know, Clare, if you really think that jacket was hers, you should take it to the cops."

I hadn't even thought of that. There might be evidence—the dirt, the tear, who knew what the cops would be able to find out. Probably nothing, but the suggestion meant Jack was innocent, right?

Except I was pretty sure the jacket wasn't done with me yet. It was like it was . . . alive, almost, in my room. I could feel its dark energy, even from miles away—or maybe that was simply my own fear.

"Yeah, I should do that," I said noncommittally. "You're sure you don't know if she was wearing it that night?"

"I never saw her again after lunch. Look, we were already kind of headed toward splitting up," Jack clarified. "I think she knew I wasn't really into her the way she wanted."

"What way is that?" I couldn't help asking.

"Amanda was all about the drama. I liked her at first

because she was so passionate about books, but then she got that way about, well, us. She wanted to spend all her time together, she wanted it to be really intense. We'd have a fight, and I'd back off for a while, and then we'd start seeing each other again. I think . . . sometimes it seemed like she wanted to block out everything by having this big relationship that would just kind of take over."

"How bad was it, really? I mean, was her dad abusive?"

"No, not like that, though they questioned him too. He was just older, and he was gone a lot for business. I met him—he was in his office, and he was kind of a dick. He barely looked up from his computer. Amanda said he hardly ever came out of his office and when he did, he was always on them for one thing or another."

It sounded kind of like Rachel's dad. He was always in his office or flying off somewhere. Rachel didn't even know exactly what his latest company did—something about collecting consumer information for online businesses.

But Rachel's dad wasn't mean. Even if he was always in a hurry, even if he used money to make up for his guilt, he did try. When he was in town, he made time for Rachel and her mom. She'd canceled plans with me once or twice when he wanted to take them to dinner or out on his sailboat. She asked me along sometimes, but I didn't think I could handle it—seeing her with her dad reminded me too much of what I was missing. Even seeing my own father a few times a year would have been a huge step up from what I had.

But I'd never stopped to consider that having him

around could have been even worse. Amanda's parents' fighting must have been really hard on her. At least with my mom, it was mostly normal. We fought, she got on my nerves, but we always made up right away.

"Do you think there's any way it could have been him?" I asked.

Jack thought for a minute. "No," he said finally. "If it was Amanda's mom who had disappeared—maybe. He really seemed to hate her. Amanda said he criticized everything about her."

Poor Amanda. Hearing Jack talk about her, she was taking shape in my mind, becoming a person rather than just an image on television or even the presence in my vision.

She'd been so gorgeous. She had perfect long brown hair that fell in waves past her shoulders, perfect wide brown eyes rimmed in eyeliner that made them seem even bigger, perfect generous lips glossed in deep pink.

"Amanda was messed up," Jack said. "I was sorry for what she was going through, but it got way too intense. I didn't want to deal with it. Look, I'm no saint, I know what I want, and when I want something I usually get it. But I never hurt Amanda."

He stared at me, barely blinking, and for a minute I almost thought he was going to kiss me. But he didn't. "Believe it or don't," he said. "If you want to know something, ask, and I'll probably tell you. But don't fuck with me again."

His words had a strange effect on me. I was irritated, but I also wanted him to touch me. Half my brain was still knotted up about Amanda and the jacket and everything else. But the other half just kept replaying what it had been like when his lips first brushed against mine, when his hands slid down my back. His revelations, his anger, hadn't dampened the way he made me feel. Even the possibility that he had hurt Amanda couldn't drown out the way I wanted him.

When he turned the key in the ignition and the old truck shuddered to life, I could have sworn he knew everything I was thinking. And even that didn't scare me the way it should have.

CHAPTER TWELVE

WE NEVER MADE IT TO THE garage sale.

A few minutes after we left the farm stand, I realized we were passing by the flea market where I bought the bag of clothes that contained the denim jacket.

"Do you mind pulling in here real quick? I just need to ask . . . something. I mean, I need to ask one of the vendors about some vintage linens she thought she'd be getting."

Jack shot me an opaque look. "You're in charge."

"You don't even have to get out of the car," I added hastily. "It'll just take a second."

Jack drove into the dirt lot, pulling up to the row of cars parked haphazardly near the pull-off. I could see the woman who sold me the clothes slouched in a folding chair with her arms crossed, wearing a different baseball cap today. I jumped out before Jack could offer to come with me, and approached her table.

"Excuse me," I said.

The woman took her time looking up at me. "Yeah?"

"Last week when I was here, I bought a bag of clothes from you for five dollars. Big Ziploc bag, it had a skirt, a pair of tights, a jacket—"

"Hey, that was 'as-is,'" the woman said quickly. "No returns."

"No, no, it's not that. I don't want to return any of it. I just wanted to ask, the jacket? It was denim, with silver buttons? I was wondering where you got it."

"Where I *got* it?" She stared at me suspiciously.

"Yes. It's . . . Well, I really like it, and it fit me perfectly, and I wondered if the person who owned it might have other things for sale."

It wasn't much of a lie, especially because there was no way the jacket would ever have fit me. But the woman's expression faded to boredom. "Can't really say. I get stuff all over the place."

I tried to keep my frustration from showing. "But maybe you would remember this. It was . . . Well, it was dirty, and torn. It had a rip in the right sleeve."

I thought I saw a brief flash of recognition pass over her face. But her expression remained unreadable, and she yawned, not bothering to cover her mouth with her hand. "I can't help it if people throw perfectly good clothes away," she said. "Just there for the taking, maybe someone else can get some use out of it. Shame to let it go to waste."

"So you found it in the trash somewhere?" I jammed my hand in my pocket, grabbing the folded bills I'd stuffed there, a couple tens. Trouble was, I didn't know how to bribe someone, and I felt my face grow hot as I smoothed the money flat on the table in front of the woman. "I think I underpaid. There were a couple of designer pieces in that bag, and I thought maybe I should give you some extra cash for them."

The woman just stared at me for a moment, then quickly picked the money up and pushed it through a hole cut in the lid of a coffee can. "Well, now you mention it, I think I found that jacket down by that landfill near the strawberry fields along Mills Peak Road."

I knew the landfill she was talking about; the official structure was surrounded by a chain link fence, but people sometimes left trash in the lot outside it. Mattresses, old tires—even just bags of trash. There were ordinances against dumping, but people ignored them when they didn't want to pay the disposal fee. The junk would make good hunting for the flea market vendors.

"You found the whole bag of clothes there?"

"No. Course not. Just the one thing, that jacket. Would have been worth a lot more if it hadn't gotten that rip."

She was right about that, anyway. Scowling at me, she set the legs of her chair down on the ground, seemingly done answering my questions; my twenty dollars hadn't gotten me much closer to the truth.

Anyone could have dumped the jacket at the landfill. It probably wasn't a bad place to leave something you were trying to get rid of; most of the garbage ended up being incinerated. Maybe whoever left it there—the person who took Amanda—hadn't wanted to risk the security cameras wired to the office shed and had just left the jacket outside the fence, counting on it to be burned or else taken by a scavenger.

Maybe not the best strategy, but I still had no idea where Amanda had been taken from, or where she'd ended up.

"Get what you needed?" Jack asked, reaching across the seat and opening the door for me.

"No. I mean, yeah, she's going to have them next week so I'll come back. Thanks for stopping. But you know, I'm thinking we should probably get back."

We barely spoke on the way home. Jack dropped me off without promising to call. I watched him drive down San Benito Road and take the hairpin turn down to the Beach Road, the vintage truck looking right at home next to all the old bungalows that lined our street.

When he was out of sight I let myself into the house. Mom was sitting at the kitchen table with her chin in her hand, a coffee cup next to her iPad, the crusts of a sandwich on a plate nearby. Her reading glasses were pushed up on her head. She'd just had her highlights touched up and her hair would have looked good if she would just quit getting it cut in the same severe corporate style. I noticed a chip in her pale pink nail polish, which I knew would drive her crazy until she could squeeze in a lunchtime manicure.

"Hi, Mom."

"Hey there, Clare-Bear."

I hadn't seen much of her this weekend between the beach party and hanging out with Rachel, and today's trip with Jack. A couple of times in the past she had gone with me on my bargain-hunting trips, and I wondered if she was feeling neglected.

My guilt mixed with frustration again—I thought it was long past time for her to start getting a social life. She'd had one in San Francisco, sort of, but it had tapered off to nothing when we moved here. When I was younger I didn't mind that she was always home with me in the evenings. In fact, I liked it. But in the last few years I'd started to resent that she didn't have more friends, the hurt looks that flitted across her face when I turned down her invitations to go to a movie or out for coffee.

"Did you call Mrs. Slade?" I asked, and I could feel her shoulders stiffen under my touch.

"I haven't had time. I've got yet another Chapter Eleven I need to prepare. . . . Honestly, Clare, if many more of my clients shut their doors I'm going to be in danger of going out of business myself."

"Who is it this time?"

"A bed-and-breakfast south of town. Really cute place, but they poured a lot of money into it a couple of years ago and with the tourism hit so hard again this year, their bookings are way down. They just can't make ends meet."

"I thought the tourist trade was supposed to be getting better. They've got all those welcome banners up downtown."

"That's the Chamber of Commerce talking." Mom sighed. "They're really hoping the holiday week will turn things around, but I'm afraid this town is going to be tainted until they catch the guy who killed those kids. I've seen the numbers, the ones they don't make public. It's pretty bad, honey."

"But it's been almost a year—"

"Did you see this?"

Mom pointed to the newspapers stacked on the table. She still subscribed to the *San Francisco Chronicle;* the headline on the front-page story read "One Year Later— Cops Are No Closer" above photos of both Dillon and Amanda. A sidebar article carried the quote "How can we keep our kids safe?" next to a picture of Winston's downtown.

"Oh, no," I said. "But that's—it's like they're *trying* to scare people."

"They just want to sell papers. Newspapers are struggling too, Clare. And it's been on the morning shows. It'll fade eventually, but . . ."

She didn't have to finish her thought. *Not soon enough,* not for the bed-and-breakfast, and maybe not for the other businesses downtown.

That reminded me of something.

"Listen, Mom, when Mrs. Granger stopped by yesterday, it was the day before her son's memorial service—it's today in Raley Park. Don't you think that's weird? That she was out running around yesterday like nothing was wrong, when it's the anniversary of Dillon's death?"

Mom looked up at me, frowning. "Well, technically, the anniversary isn't for three more days. But yes, I can see why you'd think that. But you have to understand, people grieve in all different ways."

"Do you remember her? She says she remembers you."

"I do, a little." My mom's tired features softened. "She was really sweet. I remember her selling Girl Scout cookies in front of the Frosty Top."

"My friends say Mr. Granger's crazy. Like even before Dillon died, he used to yell at the referees and get into fights at his baseball games. I guess he has a real anger problem."

"Well, it would be awfully hard to judge, I think. Are you going to the memorial?"

"I think so," I said noncommittally, hoping she wouldn't want to go.

"With Rachel?"

I thought about how drunk Rachel had been last night, how she'd been like dead weight after I used her key to unlock the front door and half-dragged her to her room. I'd been afraid her parents would hear us and come see what bad shape she was in, but the house was huge, and their rooms were in opposite wings. They never came out, and I let myself out the front after getting Rachel into bed.

Still, I'd thought I would have heard from her by now. "No, I don't think so," I hedged. "I'm going with Victoria and Giselle."

"Well, I think I'll stay here and catch up. Stick together, okay?"

There it was, the warning that went along with every conversation these days, not just in our house but all over Winston.

"We will. Giselle's parents invited people back to their house for dinner, but I'll text if we go."

"Okay, honey," Mom said, already absorbed in her work again.

. . .

An hour before the service, Rachel called to tell me that she was coming along with Giselle and Victoria. I was glad to hear from her, especially because I had nothing to wear.

"Don't worry," Rachel said. "I'll tell them to pick you up before they come over here. I have something you can borrow."

By the time the three of us got to Rachel's, her parents had already left for the service with Adrienne. We were going to be late if we didn't hurry, but as we filed up to Rachel's room she ran to get something from the kitchen.

"We can share," she said, pouring vodka over ice into a sport bottle. She added most of a can of orange soda, but it was at least two-thirds vodka. She took a healthy swig and handed it to Victoria while she dug through her closet.

I wanted to say something. It seemed completely disrespectful to be drinking at a memorial service. Giselle caught my eye and sighed. "Don't worry, Clare. I'm not drinking."

"Here," Rachel said, pulling out a simple black dress with white topstitching. It was the sort of thing she favored, tailored and short and simple. "I wore this to the JV cheer banquet last year. It'll look great on you."

She tossed it to me and I caught it—and it was like catching a handful of fire. I felt the sparkle sensation that signaled a vision, and I had the foresight to head for the bathroom adjoining Rachel's room before it took over my body completely.

This was one vision I didn't want to miss.

"I'll just change in here," I called, hoping no one noticed the quaver in my voice.

Inside her bathroom—it was larger than the one in our house, and I happened to know that Rachel's house had four and a half baths, while ours had exactly one—I sat down on the toilet and clutched the dress to my chest. My vision flickered and swam. . . . *And then I was walking through a house, the rooms large and beautiful, people laughing and talking around me.*

I was Rachel now, seeing what she saw, hearing what she heard.

I knew I was in the Stavros house because Rachel had told me they hosted the end-of-year awards banquet. I passed through the living room with its pale furniture, its glass-topped tables. I touched the handrail of a curved staircase that led upstairs. I was walking up it, my hand on the rail, my heart beating fast in my chest.

Where was I going? The party was downstairs, the laughter of all the girls echoing in my ears. But I was feeling something other than celebration. I felt . . . I concentrated, willing myself deeper into the vision, letting Rachel's emotions take over mine, letting her memories fill my mind.

I was feeling resentment. Burning envy. But why? Amanda's

house was no more opulent than Rachel's. Rachel was every bit as pretty as Amanda.

I walked into Amanda's room—deep gold walls, ruby red covers on the bed, a bookcase filled with books and knickknacks—and started going through her things. Her desk—all those papers. I fanned them out and didn't see anything that interested me. Her backpack, left lying on the floor; I searched it quickly and found only textbooks and an empty Tupperware container, remnants of some lunch that had been consumed and forgotten.

I kept going, turning my attention to the shelves. A hatbox full of hair accessories. A little silver dish that held rings and, inexplicably, a tiny glass penguin. A journal that was empty except for the first few pages, which I didn't bother to read.

Jewelry box. A smooth ebony case with five drawers, which I yanked open one by one. Necklaces, earrings, I didn't care. One, two, three—and then I opened the fourth and my eyes lit on the thing I had been searching for.

My fingers—I noticed my perfect manicure, the one Rachel was never without—picked it up delicately. A shimmering gold chain with a charm shaped like a key. Amanda's name engraved along the side in fancy letters. My heart skittered and soared. I'd found it. I would have it.

It should have been mine.

Then I was retracing my steps, shoving the necklace into my pocket, fixing a smile on my face. No one saw me. No one would know.

"Hurry up, Clare!"

Rachel's voice cut through the vision, and I hastily tugged my clothes off, leaving them in a pile on the floor.

"Just a sec," I called back. "You know, this doesn't fit after all. Do you have anything else?"

There was grumbling outside the door as I managed to hang the dress from a hook meant for a bathrobe. Rachel stuck her arm in the door, holding a navy blue dress with red piping. "You're making us late." She sighed dramatically.

But I was already tugging the dress on. I didn't even care what it looked like. All I cared about was that it had no terrible secrets to reveal about the girl I'd thought was my best friend.

. . .

We were late, but so were a lot of other people. We parked three blocks away and joined the throng trying to get to the park.

The weird thing was that, even though it seemed like half the town had shown up for the memorial, there were almost as many media people as townspeople. We counted four news vans and at least six reporters filming at various spots around the park. As I scanned the crowd, I didn't see many of the merchants who'd been working so hard on the Independence Day festival. Maybe they didn't want to add to the spectacle, staying away in an effort to take the focus off the tragedy. In three days the town would be crowded with day-trippers, and the park, downtown, and beach would be full of distractions. In addition to the food tents and the music stages, there would be a beach volleyball tournament and a parade and model airplane show and a dozen other activities. It was as if the entire population of Winston was working together to erase the history that had hung over the town, and give it a second chance.

But that was all in the future. Today, the second anniversary of Dillon's death was big news. Reporters and cameramen pressed forward toward the stage, where an older woman in white pants and a red jacket was fiddling with the microphone up at the podium. Half a dozen folding chairs were set up on the stage, and people were starting to take their seats.

"Here," Rachel said, thrusting the sports bottle at me.

"No thanks."

She shrugged and took a sip. We pressed forward with everyone else until we were in a group of people under some trees off to the left of the stage.

"Well, hello, girls," a voice called, and we all turned to see Mrs. Granger hurrying toward us. She was wearing a suit like the one she had on the other day, in a sapphire blue color that looked beautiful with her hair.

She gave us all a tired smile as she caught up to the edge of our group. "Thank you so much for coming. It means so much to me and Dillon's dad."

Mrs. Granger gave Rachel's shoulder a little squeeze, and I could have sworn Rachel winced before Dillon's mom was off to greet other people standing nearby.

Rachel took another big sip from the bottle as the woman at the podium called for attention. She asked everyone to find their seats, and people stepped out of the way to give Mrs. Granger a clear path to the stage.

"There's something very wrong with that woman," Rachel whispered loudly to me, her face flushed. I could smell the alcohol on her breath. "No one's that nice."

"Give her a break," I whispered back. "You have to give her credit for putting all of this together. Maybe it's helping her grieve or something." But deep down I had to agree; it was eerie how cheerful Mrs. Granger seemed, given that we were all assembled to observe the anniversary of her son's death.

A man in front of us turned and hushed us, frowning. On the stage, Mrs. Granger took her place next to a tall man in a dark suit—Mr. Granger, I assumed. The woman at the podium introduced herself as a local pastor and invited everyone to join her in prayer. I peeked at Victoria and Giselle and, predictably enough, Giselle's hands were folded and her head was lowered, while Victoria leaned against Rachel, the two of them looking chastened but inebriated.

The service was a short one. Mrs. Granger was remarkable, clear-voiced and even smiling as she told a story about Dillon's last baseball season. She announced that the fund that had been established in Dillon's name would be supporting a nonviolence initiative and that a tree had been planted in his memory at the elementary school. Behind her, Mr. Granger glowered and stared at the floor of the stage. When he looked out into the crowd once or twice, there was a furious intensity in his gaze that seemed to sear every face it landed on. When he looked at me, I felt a strong urge to turn away.

But then he looked at Rachel, and his expression seemed to focus even more, his mouth pinched in a tight line. She didn't notice, sipping from the bottle with her arm around Victoria, the two of them holding each other up. I tried to move in front of them to block them from Mr. Granger's gaze, but the crowd prevented me from moving.

Finally the service was over, and the crowd began to disperse. People lined up to speak to the Grangers, the reporters stepping in to snap pictures. Rachel pushed her way toward the back of the crowd, wiping her eyes before tipping up the sports bottle for the last sip.

"Do you have any idea what's gotten into her?" I asked Giselle. "I didn't know she was that upset about Dillon."

"I was going to ask you the same thing."

We managed to catch up with her, and the four of us headed back through the crowd. When we reached the car, I turned around for a final look at the people milling around the empty stage. The day was gorgeous, the sky blue, with the red, white, and blue bunting fluttering in the wind. If you didn't know better, you might think you were looking at quite a charming little town.

CHAPTER THIRTEEN

"Listen, you want to pick up takeout tonight?" Mom asked the next morning, setting down her pencil and giving me a tired smile. She'd already been working when I got up. I'd had trouble sleeping the night before, even though I came home early from Giselle's. Rachel was sleeping over there, so I knew she was in good hands, but I was worried about her and my mind raced for hours. "I'm going to have to take a break eventually."

It was on the tip of my tongue to refuse—last night everyone had been planning to get together again tonight. Everyone's parents were offering their backyards and family rooms, anxious to keep the kids together where they could keep track of them as the anniversary drew near.

But I hadn't seen Jack last night at Giselle's, and I didn't expect him to show up tonight, and I couldn't help feeling disappointed. The idea of another night of babysitting Rachel and watching Ky and Hopper pretend to beat each other up didn't hold a lot of appeal for me; maybe I'd take a night off from partying with them. Besides, it wouldn't kill me to spend a night with my mother. I could work on my corduroy pants, do a few other hand-sewing chores in front of the TV.

"That'd be cool," I said. "I've got a few things to do this afternoon. And I might go to the gym later."

"Okay. Good. Seven, maybe?"

I resisted mentioning that Nana would probably kill for a dinner invitation. Nana had only been by the house a few times in the three weeks since we moved back, mostly when Mom was gone, and I wasn't sure Mom had gone to see her at all. Once, when we were driving up along Grover Hill, I asked her exactly what it was that she couldn't forgive her mother for. I was tired of their feud; I thought I was old enough to know the big secret. But she just said it wasn't my business and that she'd have Nana over for dinner "as soon as things settled down." Given the pile of paperwork in her briefcase, that wasn't going to be any time soon.

I wondered if I should tell Nana about the vision. Maybe she could help me figure out what was going on. From what she'd told me, her gift had disappeared after she stopped responding to her own visions, and I got the feeling she didn't want anything to do with it anymore. But for something this big, this important, would she make an exception?

I pulled my phone out of my pocket and stared at it, but I didn't dial her number. For one thing, Nana was famous for forgetting to check for messages, and she didn't have a cell phone. She spent her days working in her garden or for her causes, and the best way to talk to her had always been to just show up and go looking on the grounds of the old mansion until you found her, usually crouched down next to a flower bed weeding, or pulling aphids off a rosebush.

Which I resolved to do. Soon.

I went into my room and carefully shut the door, trying to send my mom the message that I didn't want to be disturbed. I thought I'd check Facebook, maybe play a few rounds of Bubble Spinner, and then take a nap—I was exhausted from another nearly sleepless night—before I planted myself in front of the TV. The gym thing was a lie, just my way of ensuring that I'd have the afternoon to myself. Mom probably knew it, too, and I was grateful to her for not making an issue of it.

Tossing my purse onto the bed, I was about to sit down at my desk when I saw the box shoved into the closet. The tape had come loose and the flaps had popped open, revealing a flash of denim. A small but powerful jolt of urgency flashed through my body, starting in my gut and radiating out, leaving a tingle in my fingertips. An urge to dig the jacket out, touch it, hold it.

I exhaled hard, nearly overwhelmed by the force of the feeling. My mind resisted the idea—I really, really did not want to go through the painful vision again—but my body reacted independently. Without even realizing my intentions, I took a step closer.

"No," I whispered, sinking to my knees on the soft carpet. I did not have to do this.

I edged closer.

Crawling toward the box, my hand soon rested lightly on

the box flap. Inside I could see that a denim sleeve had twisted around a pair of leggings. *Close it,* I willed myself. *Close the box.*

My heart was beating faster, the tingling sensation in my fingertips increased, and now my teeth had begun to chatter. So slowly it felt like I was made of lead, I slid my fingers along the cardboard, feeling the corrugated edge flip up effortlessly. I pushed two of the flaps down, careful to avoid the material. The trembling had reached my hands now and as I folded the second set of flaps over the first, they began to shake violently. I picked up a pair of Converse sneakers and plopped them on top of the box to keep the flaps in place, and then I fell—I literally *fell* backward, pushing myself well out of the way.

I lay on my side, staring at the box, listening to the sound of my own heartbeat. I felt exhausted. Slowly, slowly some of the anxiety subsided.

I lay there until my breathing grew steady and I stopped shaking and I actually started to feel sleepy.

But a few seconds later I got back on my knees and crawled to the box, tossing the shoes onto the floor as I reached inside to grab the jacket, like I was drowning and it could save me.

· · ·

I can't say why I did it. I only know that the second my hand closed on the fabric, I understood deep in my soul that there was a message meant just for me and that I wouldn't rest until I understood it.

My vision flickered as a lurching dizziness engulfed me and I lay down again, still holding the jacket tightly. Under my fingertips I felt the weave, the folds of the fabric, but then they seemed to melt and grow warm, turning into something pliable and soft. Alive.

The feeling of horror, the buzzing electric thrill of fear. I vaguely felt tears spilling down my cheeks. Silver sparkles danced and began to settle, like the flakes inside a snow globe, falling into place to form an image.

At first I couldn't make it out clearly. Darkness, little spots of light, a wavery white rectangle. Then the sensation in my hands returned—sort of. Except instead of holding the fabric I was now holding something hard and square in my right hand and my left—

My left hand rested on a steering wheel. For now, in this moment, I was Amanda, and I was driving.

I glanced down at my other hand and I was holding a cell phone. That was the glowing rectangle—the phone's face. My thumb moved over the keys, typing something one letter at a time—and I was much faster and better at it than I was in real life.

I KNOW U CD WEAR ME OUT

Somewhere deep inside my mind I felt rather than heard the ding of the message being sent, and then my thumb was moving again.

I M TOUCHING

And then the whoosh of terror as I felt myself being thrown against the door, slamming my knee against the handle. I'd driven off the road, and I hit the brakes. The phone fell from my hand as I gripped the steering wheel hard, yanking it to the left as the darkness outside my windshield took shape and I saw the road again, angling in front of me. A shadow crossed my headlights as I drove back onto the road, crossing a steep shoulder. Was that the bump? The lurch? Had I hit something?

Get out, *the part of my brain that was still me urged.* Get out and make sure everything's okay. *But that voice barely registered. The panic and fear and adrenaline inside me escalated as I cursed under my breath, and again there was no sound, just the rushing of my mind.*

Fuck.

The word had barely passed my lips when everything rushed away from me again, replaced by raw terror.

Pain.

Oh my God it hurt, the feeling of my skull being cleaved in two, my heart crushed against my ribs from the inside, electric shocks racing up and down my nerve endings—all twined together with a terror like I'd never known, a fear so great and terrible that I felt like my soul—Amanda's soul?—was being savagely yanked from me. What is it what is it what is it, *my own mind clamored, desperate to understand what was happening, but there were no answers, there was just the dark slicing through the smashed shards of what I'd seen, as though it had been a screen that shattered with the last frame frozen in place. The car was stopped; everything was silent. The road, the phone, my hand, the glow of the dashboard, all mixed up and broken, and in their place a pain that grew along with fear until I thought I would explode. I was screaming as loud as I could and heard nothing, nothing at all, because my breath had been stolen away and there was only my weak heartbeat as everything finally, mercifully, disappeared.*

CHAPTER FOURTEEN

THIS TIME CONSCIOUSNESS RETURNED more slowly, in little surges, as I was lying on the floor again. The vision was over, the jacket lying crumpled next to me. My fingers were curled around nothing, and I wondered how I had finally managed to let go.

I felt weak and sick, like I'd survived a long bout of the flu and was still feverish and parched. I moved my fingers just to make sure I still could, my head throbbing as my eyes tracked their movement. The pain was different from other visions; in the borrowed memories I'd struck my knee, but it was my head that had felt like it was splitting. It was as though part of the vision was too much to absorb, as though I couldn't fully grasp what I'd seen and I'd blocked it instead, but blocking it had taken a toll on my body. I couldn't fight the visions, and this was what I'd gotten for trying.

Pushing myself carefully upright, the blood rushed from my face and my stomach lurched, a wave of nausea passing through me. The bars of sunlight from my window had moved across the carpet, and I knew I had been out longer this time. I glanced at the clock on my bedside table—2:18. How long had it been? Half an hour? More?

I stared at the pile of blue fabric. What would happen if I touched it now? I hadn't resisted the vision this time; I'd let it come, tried to see it through to find out how it ended—and still it had been interrupted. By what or who, I didn't know. I didn't have the strength to try and fight the searing pain again and I guessed that even if I did, I wouldn't get any farther than I already had.

Which was . . . where? The first time I'd seen darkness dappled with spots of light. Something that might have been the inside of the car. And then the vision had changed and I had seen a face—the furious face of a woman, threatening me, screaming at me.

This time I'd seen more—the phone, the message Amanda had been writing—and something else had happened. I'd run off the road. I'd bottomed out or hit something, or else it was a bigger drop than I'd realized. I'd yanked the wheel and gotten the car back on the road.

I shuddered at what I had to do next. I couldn't leave the jacket on the floor like that. I got the tongs again, along with a large Ziploc bag. I fished up the jacket and dropped it into the bag, sealing it carefully to make sure I didn't touch the fabric. Holding it through the plastic, I felt no resistance.

I had to find out more about that night. Jack had told me what he knew, which was basically nothing—he'd received her texts but hadn't answered them; he didn't know she was missing until the next day. He didn't know where she had ended up or what had happened. And I didn't know anyone else who'd been friends with Amanda.

But . . .

Tucked into the drawer of the wooden table in the hall, where Mom kept a dish for her keys and a glass jar full of pretty shells, was a thin Yellow Pages. Why they still printed phone books I had no idea—no one I knew ever looked up numbers in them. But when we moved into the house the book was sitting on the porch in a plastic wrapper, and Mom hadn't thrown it out.

STAVROS. It wasn't hard to find—G. Stavros, 515 Elderberry Circle. I knew exactly where that was, one of several roads that made up the newer, wealthy neighborhood high up along the ridge overlooking the ocean. It had been built since we moved away, an enclave of a few dozen houses that had views of both the ocean below and the flat lands to the east. In my opinion the views weren't as nice as my grandmother's, but if you wanted new construction, it was the best in town.

I changed into my gym clothes—baggy shorts from gym class at Blake, plus a sports bra and tank top. I stuffed the plastic bag containing the jacket into my backpack and threw my water bottle and iPod in, too, for authenticity's sake. I needn't have bothered, though: Mom was gone. "Went to the office," said the note she'd left me.

The ride wasn't an easy one, and I was sweating and breathing hard by the time I got to Elderberry Circle. The houses here were even more spectacular than I expected. Front lawns were landscaped with rock gardens and flower beds and neatly trimmed trees. Driveways were paved with brick and stone, and front doors featured gleaming brass hardware.

Number 515 was the second from the top, a traditional redbrick mansion with black shutters and a covered front porch. But there were signs of neglect. The lawn was neatly trimmed, but the flower beds were overgrown, the few bushes growing out of control. Mounds of dirt were evidence that gophers had attacked the grass, and one of the windows on the lower floor had a cracked pane that had been fixed with clear tape. Several yellow sticky notes were also stuck to the front door.

Leaning my bike against the mailbox, I walked up the drive with a sense of dread. What was I thinking? Why would Amanda's mother want to talk to me—or anyone— about her missing daughter? Wouldn't I just add to her pain, coming here like this?

But if there was a chance, even a small one, that I could help her find out what had happened to Amanda, wasn't it worth it?

I was about to knock on the front door when it opened, making me jump. A pale, narrow face stared out at me from the crack and then disappeared. A moment later the chain was unfastened and the door opened wider.

"What," the person standing in front of me mumbled. "What do you want."

I took a step back. "I—I'm Clare Knight. My mother is Susan Knight."

She stared at me for so long, I thought she wasn't going to speak again. She finally said, "You're Susie's girl," and opened the door some more.

At first she looked like a girl barely older than me, but as I followed her into the house I realized that her hair—wavy and long, almost down to her waist—was streaked with gray. Her skin was smooth and pale, but there were wrinkles at the corners of her eyes and around her mouth. Her lips were thin and dry, almost bloodless, and her eyelashes were so light you could barely see them, making her big blue eyes seem even bigger, almost freakishly so. The smell of liquor hit me hard.

"Um, are you Mrs. Stavros?"

"You can call me Heaven. If you want."

We passed through rooms decorated with expensive, dusty furniture, and I recognized it from my vision, the night of the cheer dinner. Amanda had still lived in this house then; so had her father. Her mother had not yet become this lifeless husk. I followed her into the kitchen, which smelled unexpectedly nice, like tomato sauce and lemon. On the counter were a couple of grocery bags. One was leaking onto the granite, a dark spreading puddle. Mrs. Stavros went to the microwave and popped open the door, yelping when she tried to lift the contents, a plastic tray containing a reheated meal.

"Damn!" she said. "You know, Mandy used to like these.

I cooked her a real meal every day, and for her father whenever he could be bothered to come home. But the two of them never could seem to get to the table on time. . . ."

She dug into a drawer and came up with a dish towel, gingerly carrying it over to the table. Then she looked at me and wiped her hands on her pants. They were a nice pair of linen cargo pants, but they hung on her; I guessed she hadn't always been as reed-thin as she was now. She left a smear of tomato sauce on the fabric but didn't seem to notice. "Do you want one? I have lasagna and sesame chicken—lasagna was Amanda's favorite."

"No thank you, Mrs. Stavros. I mean . . . Heaven."

"Do you want something to drink? A soda? Tea?"

I was thirsty from the ride but I didn't want to ask her for anything. In the fluorescent light of the kitchen fixture, she looked almost sick, the smudges under her eyes taking on a purple shade, her cheeks hollowed and her shoulders hunched. She looked more than thin—she looked beaten. But she stared at me intensely, her eyes bright and unblinking as we sat across from each other. Folding her hands on her lap, the meal forgotten, she leaned forward. Her intense gaze made me uncomfortable and I snuck a look around. The kitchen looked clean at first, but then I noticed the overflowing garbage bag leaning against the cabinets. Maybe a friend or a relative brought groceries and did a little cleaning, but Mrs. Stavros had forgotten to put the groceries away. By the look of whatever was melting, it had been a while.

I could see into the family room next to the kitchen. It

was a much different story in there. The drapes were closed, and the television—a large flat-screen taking up most of the wall over a stone fireplace—was on, the sound muted. A nest of blankets and pillows lay on the couch and I wondered if Mrs. Stavros had been sleeping there. All around were empty plates and boxes of Kleenex, magazines and clothes abandoned on the floor.

I felt really sad, seeing what her life was like. Still missing her daughter. Nearly a year of not knowing where Amanda was or what had happened to her.

"Mrs. Stavros . . . I think I might have something that belonged to your daughter."

"You do?" She blinked, looking both curious and confused. That was when I spotted the vodka jug on the counter, one of the big ones like the boys occasionally brought to the beach. The liquid level was only a few inches and I wondered how much of it she'd had today.

I pulled the plastic bag out of my backpack. Inside, the jacket was tightly wadded; you could barely tell what it was.

I handed the bag to Mrs. Stavros, not wanting to touch the jacket. "I think this might have been hers."

She set the bag on the table. Then she let out a cry, yanking it savagely against her face, pressing the plastic to her cheeks.

"No," she sobbed in a cracked voice.

I suddenly felt like I'd made a terrible mistake. I hadn't come here to torture her. "I'm sorry. I'm sorry. I can go, if—"

"This was Mandy's. Where did you get it? Where?" Mrs. Stavros laid the jacket carefully out on the table, smoothing down the wrinkled fabric, touching the buttons and tracing the lines of stitching with her fingertips.

"I . . . found it. A woman was selling things. Out by the power plant, where they have the flea market on the weekends. She had a table. . . ."

But Mrs. Stavros wasn't listening. She was making a sound deep in her throat, a kind of low moan. "I remember when we bought this," she said in a voice barely above a whisper.

"You're sure it's hers, then?"

"Oh, yes. It was a limited-edition piece, they made less than a hundred. We were up in the city last summer . . . Mandy's dad had gone back to Greece, so I took her for a little trip to celebrate the end of the school year. Just us girls, a shopping spree. There's a Ripley Couture boutique on Stockton, by Union Square. . . ."

I knew where she was talking about—the most expensive shopping district in the city.

"Mrs. Stavros," I said, deciding to take a chance. "Did anything else that belonged to Amanda disappear around that time? Maybe a necklace, a charm on a gold chain?"

She looked at me in confusion. "Yes, but—how would you know about that? It was her favorite, the one she got when she joined Gold Key. She loved that necklace. The only time she took it off was for cheer, because they weren't allowed to have jewelry during performances. Did you find that, too?"

"No, I'm sorry."

Rachel had stolen Amanda's Gold Key necklace after being refused membership.

Then Amanda disappeared. And Rachel was accepted into the club. The one she was now running for president of. The one her mother was obsessed with. The one whose exclusion had made her feel like a failure.

I remembered the emotions I had felt during the vision—the humiliation mixed with rage. That couldn't have been enough, though, could it? Enough to hurt Amanda? Enough to kill her? Just to take her place in the club?

"Oh, well, then. I remember everything about that day in the city. We bought a few things, got our nails done, had tea at the Westin," Mrs. Stavros murmured. "We had such a wonderful time."

Two thin tears trickled out of the corners of her eyes, making their way down her pale cheeks and splashing down onto her lap without her seeming to notice. She'd forgotten the necklace already, but I wanted to kick myself for adding to her pain.

"You say you got this at the flea market?" she said, tapping the jacket. Her eyes were so pale they were nearly colorless. "How did it get there?"

"I don't know. I was hoping, I thought maybe you could tell me. Do you think she was wearing it, um . . ." I couldn't bring myself to say "on the night she disappeared."

"Everyone makes mistakes," she blurted out. "Mandy never wanted to . . . One time, she stepped on a snail, out in the garden, and she cried. Over a *snail*. Her dad, he didn't understand her. She always wanted a pet, but George wouldn't hear of it. Just a kitten, I said, something of her very own. Because she didn't have any sisters or brothers. I always hoped . . ."

She was fading back into her memories, making less and less sense. Alcohol and grief had taken away her ability to reason.

"Did she call you? The night she . . . When she was out, did you hear from her at all?"

"She called that boy, Jack Dimaunahan. The police told me that. She'd had lunch with him that day."

"What about earlier? Do you know what she did between lunch and when she went out again that night?"

"She came home. She was in her room all afternoon. She took a shower around dinnertime. I know because she left her towel on the floor. I could never get her to remember to hang it back up." She flashed a brief, sad smile at the memory. "She wanted to go see Jack, but her dad and I didn't like for her to date during the week, even in the summer. I was strict that way. So she called some girlfriend. They were going to get lattes. We went to bed after she left."

"Who did she call?"

For a moment, Mrs. Stavros's eyes seemed to focus, and she frowned. "Why are you asking me all this?"

"I, uh . . ." I thought fast. "It's just that after I found her jacket, some of the kids were talking about Amanda. How much everyone misses her. It seems like she was really special."

I felt guilty, playing on Mrs. Stavros's grief this way, but it was the only thing I could think of to keep her talking.

"She was," Mrs. Stavros said softly. "So special. My little girl."

"So she called someone that night. Do you remember who it was?"

"I wish I knew. I heard voices in the foyer—I thought maybe one of her friends in the neighborhood had stopped by, or someone could have gotten dropped off, or walked from down the hill."

"Did the police try to find out who she was with?"

"Of course. They did all kinds of interviews, but they could never find anyone who said they'd been to our house that night. That's one of the reasons they suspected she was on her way to meet Jack. They suggested we had imagined the voices." She sighed. "And maybe we did. It's been so long, so many times I've gone over that night in my mind. But you know, I never thought it was that boy. He was a child. They both were."

I thought of Rachel again. Lately I didn't know if anyone would think she was a child. It wasn't just the drinking and the recklessness—it was like something had changed in her eyes, like they were emptier.

Rachel had changed. But it had happened before I ever came back to Winston. She'd just been hiding it for the last few weeks. All the time we had spent laughing and talking together, creating a business and hanging out with

our friends, there was something else underneath the surface, something that was eating away at her.

Maybe, if I was a better friend, I would have recognized
it right away—that the fun-loving, generous girl I'd always
known was in trouble.

And maybe, just maybe, she had never been that girl at all.

CHAPTER FIFTEEN

"How are you?" I asked, pressing the phone against my ear and trying to sound solicitous. I'd left Mrs. Stavros sitting in her kitchen, sipping at the straight vodka she poured into a juice glass as I was saying good-bye. I had biked to the little park by the elementary school and parked under a shady tree before I called Rachel.

"Not great," she said in a strained voice. "I feel like I could sleep for a week. And I probably should, but we're leaving for Monterey tomorrow night, and Dad's yelling at everyone to get packed."

"Oh, yeah, I forgot about that." Rachel's parents didn't want to stay in town for the Fourth; they didn't like being around when the town was overrun with tourists. Going to Monterey didn't seem like much of a solution, since it was bound to be just as crazy up there, but that was what they'd decided to do. According to Rachel, her mom had made the reservations ages ago. "It's no wonder you're tired. You've been partying for two days straight."

"Yeah. Look. I already feel like shit. If you just called to judge me—"

"No, no, I'm sorry." I took a deep breath. "I'm worried about you, that's all. You haven't been acting like yourself."

Rachel was silent for a moment and then she mumbled, "I know," so softly I almost didn't hear her.

"Listen," I said. "I saw Mrs. Stavros. She says—"

"Where did you see her? She *never* comes out of her house anymore."

"She says Amanda went out for lattes the night she disappeared. With a *girlfriend*. Look, can I come over? I really have to talk to you."

This time the pause was even longer. I was sweating more than I had on the uphill trip.

"All right," Rachel finally said. "But Adrienne's got piano this afternoon so it'll have to be quick."

· · ·

When she met me at the door, she seemed to be feeling better.

"Okay, look," she said, when we were in her room with the door shut. "Amanda used to use me as an excuse. Whenever she wanted to see Jack, she'd say she was with me. I'd walk over to her house, and then she'd drop me off at home and go do whatever she wanted."

Clearly my best friend knew a lot more than she had

told me. "You said you didn't know Amanda very well. Remember? You said you hardly ever talked to her."

"Well, we *were* on cheer together. So yeah, we talked. But, you know, we didn't *talk* talk. Just after practice and whatever."

I thought of mentioning the necklace, but I was afraid Rachel would shut me down if I pushed her too far. I tried to think of a way to guide the conversation. "Were you . . . jealous of her?"

Rachel raised her eyebrows. "Jealous? Why, because of Jack?" She laughed derisively. "Please. What's with this weird fixation of yours, anyway?"

"Well, the other day you said you thought you were next. That you were afraid you were going to be killed. So, you know, I care about whether you live long enough to start junior year with me."

Rachel blushed. "Forget about that, okay? I was drunk. I was just . . . messing around."

"I don't know, you seemed pretty scared to me for real. Look, Rachel, it's *me* you're talking to. If you're in trouble, if something's going on, you can tell me, okay?"

"I asked you to drop it." Twin spots of color appeared on her cheeks as she bit her lip, staring at the floor. Whatever was going on, it had her shaken up.

"But it also turns out you knew Amanda a lot better than you said you did. Things aren't adding up, Rachel."

She looked up, her eyes boring into mine, sparking with

anger . . . and fear. "Okay, and you've been keeping things from *me*, too. What the hell is that about?"

"What do you mean?"

"With Jack? Lara said she saw you in his truck, over at the flea market. What were you doing there? With *him*?"

I sighed. "I like him, okay? I'm sorry I haven't kept you posted on every little thing I do, but it has nothing to do with any of this." Which wasn't a lie. I hoped.

"But I keep telling you he's trouble. He's dangerous, Clare. You know those convenience store robberies last winter?"

"No, because I wasn't here. I was living in San Francisco, remember?"

"I'm just saying, they never caught the guy who was doing it. It could have been Jack—it was right after he did all that other stuff. He had a gun, Clare."

I laughed, because she was getting into ridiculous territory. "*Someone* had a gun, maybe. Not Jack."

"He's nothing but trash."

Her words stung. I thought about how Winston was divided into haves and have-nots—maybe I could slum it with the rich kids, but there was no confusion as to which side Jack was on. "Well, you're a snob," I said. "And a liar, and a thief, so I wouldn't be talking."

"What the hell are you talking about?"

"Nothing," I said, avoiding her eyes. If I told her I knew about the necklace, I'd have to tell her about the visions, too. "Forget I said it."

"You know what, maybe you should go," Rachel said, getting to her feet. "Maybe you ought to spend a little time figuring out who your real friends are."

I walked by myself to the front door of her house, my footsteps echoing on expensive marble floors. I'd never felt quite so alone.

CHAPTER SIXTEEN

THERE WAS ONE PERSON IN WINSTON who I could count on to be honest with me, someone who hadn't lied to me yet. Someone I'd been taking for granted for far too long.

After I left Rachel's house, I pedaled my bike back across town and up Grover Hill, where the widow's walk on top of my grandmother's house rose high above all the other roofs in the neighborhood, a wooden structure with the ocean laid out below like a brilliant blue carpet dotted with fluttering white sails.

When we lived in the city, Mom would get irritable for days before one of Nana's rare visits. She'd polish the silver and get the good china out, then disappear into the kitchen so she wouldn't have to make conversation when Nana arrived.

I couldn't say that things were ever exactly *good* between Mom and Nana as far back as I could remember, but they used to be tolerable. When I was little, Mom used to drop me off at Nana's house a couple of days a week, and we would spend the day playing together. It never seemed strange to me at the time, but now I realized that not every grandmother would be willing to get down on the floor and play with Play-Doh and blocks and dolls and Barbie castles, Playmobil pirate ships and dress-up clothes and toy kitchens. But Nana acted just like a kid herself, pretending to make grilled cheese sandwiches and serving them to stuffed animals, or tying gauzy scarves around herself so that she too could be a superhero and run around the backyard with me "rescuing" her spotted mutt, Peaches.

But best of all was "make-stuff time"—Nana's term for it—when we went into the creative room, which was another one of her peculiar names for things, sat on the floor, and did crafts. My favorite was sewing. As soon as I got old enough to hold a needle and use sharp sewing scissors, I was making projects—an uneven pillow stuffed with shredded foam, a potholder made from layers of old quilts stitched together, a doll dress created from the sleeve of a blouse with holes cut out for arms. Nana always complimented my creations and put them into service. The leftover bits were pinned to the curtains in the creative room, until there were dozens of lumpy, odd little fabric treasures all the way to the floor.

I remembered those curtains when I hung my wares from the sides of the NewToYou stand. It was like being back with Nana on a lazy afternoon, without a care in the world.

Now, as I got off my bike and pushed, rather than struggle to ride up the last steep section of road, I thought about the last time Mom and I went to Nana's house, to say good-bye before moving to the city all those years ago. A big box waited by the door. Inside was Nana's sewing machine, the wonderful old Bernina, though I didn't know it at the time. But Mom must have known, because she tried to leave it.

"Well, I'll let you know when I get the new phone number," Mom had said, after an awkward good-bye.

Nana had nodded matter-of-factly, finally accepting that she'd failed to talk Mom out of moving. Whatever the nature of their huge fight—and Mom always refused to tell me, saying it was "private"—Nana must have known she would make things worse by continuing to beg Mom to change her mind.

She could not, however, resist pulling Mom into one of her bone-crushing hugs. I remember my mom didn't hug back, which I thought was weird. Her hands, one of them tightly holding her car keys, hung at her sides as she squeezed her eyes shut, grimacing until Nana finally let go.

"This is for Clare," Nana had said, picking up the box, which was obviously heavy. "I'll just take it out to the car for you."

"Mom, what on earth is that? I don't have room—"

"Now, now, you can put it in a closet until she's older," Nana interrupted. "It's just a few things she likes. It'll keep her busy so you can get settled in."

That had gotten Mom's attention. I saw her hesitate, her eyes narrowed, considering. "Well . . . What's in there? I definitely don't need any more junk."

Nana got most of her toys from garage sales. It drove

Mom crazy because Nana had plenty of money and could afford to buy all new things, but she felt it was irresponsible to buy more possessions that would just end up cluttering landfills when other people were getting rid of perfectly good things. Mom had always been leery of other people's germs and I remember she would make me scrub my hands the minute I got home from a playdate at Nana's.

But Nana had just laughed. "No, no junk, I promise."

She'd won that round. Later, when Mom was busy unpacking and setting up our apartment, I opened the box myself and discovered that Nana had given me her sewing machine. By the time Mom found me, I was pretending to sew the towels from the bathroom—Nana had wisely removed the needle and presser foot and anything else I could hurt myself on—and I was so engrossed in it that she let me keep it in my room, where it would end up staying for the next six years. Other things changed—my walls were painted a few times and my ruffled Pocahontas bedspread was replaced with a coverlet of my own design—but the sewing machine was always there.

I reached the top of the hill and started down Nana's street, wishing I'd told her how much that sewing machine meant to me. I supposed she probably knew, since I made every birthday and Christmas gift on it. I'd sent the last one on her birthday in March, a matching eyeglasses case and journal cover made from strips of colorful silk neckties, and she'd written me a gushing thank-you note in her looping handwriting on bright orange stationery.

Still, my steps slowed as I got close to the house. I didn't know where to start, how to apologize. I was struggling with my thoughts, taking my time propping up my bike against the trunk of a giant magnolia tree, when I heard her call my name.

"Clare! Precious! Is that *you*?"

She sounded so delighted that I felt my misgivings evaporate. I followed the sound of her voice, spotting her leaning out a second-story window.

"Nana!"

"Front door's open, honey—I'll race you!"

The front door was not only open, but ajar, so anyone could have walked in and robbed her blind, as my mother would have said. A canvas bag full of fresh-cut flowers was lying on a rusting round table on the porch, along with a pair of pruners and a single flowered garden glove. Nana had no doubt forgotten them there, and I picked up the flowers so they wouldn't wilt in the heat.

Meeting me at the bottom of the stairs, Nana hugged me just as hard as always, and I breathed in her signature spicy perfume mixed with something salty and traces of sweat. Her T-shirt—"Save the Loggerheads!" printed on the front over a picture of a turtle—had rings of sweat under the arms, and when she finally pulled away from me she brushed dirt off the front. "Sorry, I must look like I crawled out of a barn. I've been in the garden. Peaches dug up a dead squirrel and lord, that was a mess. . . . Are you hungry?"

She was talking as fast as ever, grinning from ear to

ear, and it was hard to resist smiling back. For a moment I just looked at her, not worrying about what other people might think of her in her crazy shirt and flowing skirt that appeared to be some sort of sheer organza layered over a shiny fabric.

"Oh!" she said. "Lester brought the most delicious muffin. I don't think I ate it all yet. . . . Come on into the kitchen."

I followed her through the house, noting with relief that nothing looked very different. The furniture had been moved around, but that was nothing new—Nana was always deciding that the energies would be better if a sofa got the afternoon light or a game table was moved under a window to display photos. It was the same old mix of beautiful antiques from her second husband, and quirky pieces she picked up at tag sales. I could hear my mother tsking that there was way too much furniture in the rooms, and I had to agree—not just furniture, but knick-knacks, paintings, photographs, books, and objects I couldn't identify—but that was nothing new either.

The kitchen was tidy, a flowered cloth draped on the old wooden table. Nana got a plate from the white marble counter and squinted at it. "I'm afraid I took a bite, but it still looks pretty good. Wanna try?"

I was going to say no but the muffin looked amazing, crusted with sparkling sugar and studded with bright red raspberries, and I couldn't resist. "Mmmm," I said with my mouth full. "Lester can sure bake, whoever he is."

"Oh, he didn't make these. He bought them at Plaisir," Nana said, naming the fanciest bakery in town. "He's trying to impress me and I'm taking advantage of it."

Mom didn't like to talk about Nana's gentleman callers, as she referred to them. I used to worry that they were after her money, and maybe Nana did too, because they never lasted long, but she did seem to enjoy their attention.

"So . . . ," she said, staring at me intensely. "What's up?"

"Um . . . I kind of have a problem."

"Mmm-hmm." She waited, her eyes bright and crafty, giving me an encouraging smile. I heard Peaches somewhere far off in the gardens, probably barking at a bird or a rabbit.

"With, you know, the gift. I saw something."

Now the mirth disappeared from Nana's eyes and she was suddenly very serious. "All right. Tell me."

"You know how you told me I could stop, if I wanted? That if I never did anything about the visions, never tried to make anything right, they'd go away?"

"Yes . . ."

"I wish I had." I felt the start of tears, hot and stinging. If only I'd let it die away, I wouldn't have gotten sucked into things that were over my head, that had nothing to do with me. I could be working on my tan and spending my time on my business and my social life, rather than trying to solve a mystery that kept getting more and more complicated.

"Oh, honey. I wish I knew what to tell you."

"Do you ever wish you hadn't let the gift go?"

"No," Nana answered sharply. And then a minute later,

in a much softer tone, "And sometimes yes. You know, when you first told me you had the gift, I was so proud. Can you believe that? Something that bound you to me, my most precious grandchild . . ."

I automatically thought, *Your only grandchild,* as I had when I was little. She always called me her favorite, and I'd remind her I was her only one. Of course I liked it that way, liked knowing I got all of her attention.

"I never understood how it skipped my sisters, skipped your mother . . . I thought it had died out. I knew Alma's death caused her descendants to inherit this strange gift somehow, but after two generations, I figured that would be it. Then when you used to grab your grandpa Quinn's old coat and tell me you wanted to ride in the blue car . . . Well, that was when I suspected you had it."

I didn't remember a coat, didn't remember a blue car. And I had never known either of my grandfathers, not Quinn—the love of Nana's life, who died in Vietnam—or Doyle, the rich one who'd conveniently died after they'd been married thirteen years, leaving her the Raley mansion and the fortune that went with it.

Nana must have noticed my puzzlement. "Quinn had a Bel Air convertible he just loved . . . used to drive it along Highway One. Quinn drank too much and drove too fast and one Friday night he hit a man who was walking home along the side of the road, a laborer. There wasn't anything for it, and Quinn was devastated. I always thought that would be what killed him, not the war—I sold that car to the first person who made an offer after he died, and was glad to be rid of it. But the jacket—lambskin, soft as butter—I couldn't bear to throw it out. Used to hang it by the back door, wear it if I needed to go out in the fog. . . . Anyway." Nana shook her head as though shaking away cobwebs of memory. "You and the blue car. That was when I knew."

"Nana. It isn't *normal*. I mean, did it ever occur to you to see someone? A . . ." *Psychiatrist? Doctor? Researcher?* I realized how ridiculous it sounded. After all, I'd never told anyone besides her and Mom.

"And become a curiosity? Someone to be studied, like those poor twin baby girls joined at the head, or someone who can memorize a whole book word for word? No thank you, Clare," Nana said with conviction. "I never wished that for myself and certainly not for you. That's why when you stopped telling me about it, I thought maybe it was for the best."

"I stopped telling you because Mom *made* me," I blurted out, angry tears threatening to spill from my eyes.

Nana looked stricken. "Oh, honey . . . When was that?"

"When I was in grade school." I bit my lip, remembering.

"Tell me what happened. Please."

"I liked my teacher a lot. Ms. Applethorn—she was young and fun. She used to let me borrow her orange vest to help with recess supervision. One day I put on the vest and I felt how happy she was and I saw her kissing Mr. Clay, the principal. I was so excited because I thought they would get married and—anyway, I came home from school and told Mom."

"And?"

"And . . ." I sighed, remembering. "Turns out Mr. Clay was married already and his wife was pregnant with their second child. Not that I knew it at the time. All I knew was that Mom freaked. She made me swear that I would not tell anyone what I knew. Not Ms. Applethorn, and especially not Mr. Clay, none of my friends . . . not you or Dad either. *No one.* She was really angry."

"Oh . . . honey." Nana's expression sagged.

"And then she told me I had to stop reading the stories in people's clothes. I told her I didn't think I could, and she . . . She took both my hands and squeezed them hard, hard enough that I started to cry, and she got really, *really* close to me so I couldn't look away and she said *yes you can.* She repeated it like three times and then she made me promise again. I was afraid if I didn't, she would . . . punish me and get mad all over again."

But that wasn't the truth. The thing I worried about when Mom talked to me that day, her face inches away from mine and her voice deadly serious, was that she would stop loving me if I didn't do what she asked. I'd never seen her so upset about anything. I had almost wished she'd punish me, spank me, ground me—but she had just stared at me for the longest time until she finally seemed satisfied that I meant my promise, and let go.

"Clare . . . Clare, I am so sorry. So sorry that you had to

make that promise and so sorry that . . . You know, when I was younger I used to think it was a blessing, something that made me special. I wasn't particularly careful with it. I used it to know things about other people, their secrets . . . I thought it was a good thing, a way to get close to people."

She pushed a few strands of gray hair out of her face and they promptly fell right back down again.

"Your grandpa Quinn—he knew what I could do. In fact, it was what brought us together. I caught him cheating at cards, you see. He took me out and stole a kiss, and I touched his jacket and suddenly understood why he always had a pocket full of money, but I couldn't resist. I've always loved the bad boys."

"Nana!"

"Well, I can't help it, darlin'."

I had never thought about what it was like for Nana trying to raise a child on her own, having lost her husband. Of course she'd tried to protect my mom—it was just the two of them, at least until Nana remarried.

"And then one day I made a mistake," she continued, subdued. "I told your mother something about her best friend. I don't even remember what it was anymore, nothing terrible, some little thing girls did. You see, I never made a secret of it with your mama, what I could do. And she got so angry with me. She must have been about your age, and . . . Well, I hadn't noticed that she'd practically grown up on me. Doyle was gone by then, and I was learning to live alone, and here your poor mama just wanted to be like all the other girls. And it was hard, with us living up here in this big old house. . . . Anyway, she barely spoke to me for a week. Told me if I didn't stop prying—because that was how she saw it, you see, touching other people's clothing and prying into things that weren't my business— then she was going to run away, and I'd never see her again."

Nana's eyes were red and watery. She grabbed a dish-cloth that was folded over the back of a chair, dabbed her eyes, and cleared her throat. I tried to picture my mother at my age, but I could barely imagine Mom young. I could certainly imagine her being angry at Nana, since she seemed to have been furious with her forever.

"I was so scared," Nana whispered. "I'd buried two husbands and I couldn't stand the thought that I might lose my daughter too."

She'd given up the gift. She had once been like me, able to read clothes, the fabric that she held in her hands, and she had stopped. All because my mother had asked her to.

And that meant I should be able to stop, too. Put this behind me and pretend I'd never been different, never been this way, be a completely normal girl. It might be hard for a while, since what I loved most was working with vintage clothing—but I could switch to using only new materials, fabric and trims off the bolt. There was no reason I had to come in contact with other people's castoffs. I could start fresh, sell the rest of my creations dirt cheap next Saturday and use some of my earnings to buy supplies. I'd taken a pattern-making class; I had a portfolio of designs all ready, and ideas for thousands more.

There were a dozen different reasons for me to put an

end to my gift, and only one—well, two—why I shouldn't. First, I truly loved working specifically with vintage things, thinking about the history of a garment as I sewed. And second . . .

Second was wrapped in a plastic bag and jammed in my backpack. I'd taken it with me when I left Mrs. Stavros in an attempt to save her from painful memories. But I also knew that the denim jacket—and the terrible story that went with it—was not ready to let me go.

"Nana," I said haltingly, "I—I can't. I just can't stop yet. There's this . . . Something happened."

And then suddenly I was telling her everything. Finding the box at the flea market, the clothes tumbling to the floor, the denim jacket seeming to draw me closer. The terrible sensations when I touched the fabric the second time, the vision of the darkened interior of a car, the lurching, the impact. I told her about going driving with Jack in his truck, and the vision with Rachel and the necklace, and my visit with Mrs. Stavros. Nana listened to all of it without interrupting, holding my hand in her surprisingly strong, cool one, her eyes intent on mine.

"I don't know what to do," I said. "I wish . . ."

I hesitated, aware of how selfish what I was about to say would sound.

"You wish it would just go away," Nana said softly. "It's in the past, and at this point it's pretty clear that Amanda is never coming back, and people have moved on, except for her poor mother."

"Yes," I whispered.

Like when I would make a castle down at the beach as a little girl with my mom—the same beach where I now went with my friends on Saturdays to party. I used to love making complicated castles with bridges and moats, sticks and shells for decoration.

But if I made my castle too close to the water—and I always built it too close to the water—eventually the tide would creep up the beach. The waves would lap at the base of my castle, nibbling away at it, and each time they would come farther. Sand would start to seep into my gullies and moats, and the details would be melted away until one big wave would come and immerse the whole thing, leaving a sodden lump where my beautiful castle had been.

Amanda's disappearance was like that. There was a reason people didn't speak about her. It was too sad, too scary for those left behind to think about how vulnerable we all really were.

"Honey, you *can* quit, if you want to. But . . . it's harder than you might think. The first time I tried, I failed. I started up again, almost without even knowing I was doing it. Just little things, a vision here and there, strangers I ran into at the market or at church. And I hardly ever did anything about them. I had a busy life. You came along, and even if your mom and I had our differences, we were happy then. You and your folks visited me all the time; I thought nothing could hurt our family. And then . . . Well, you don't need to know the details. But something happened. I—

noticed something, something that I wasn't meant to see. It put a question in my mind and the way these things do, it nagged at me and grew until I couldn't stand it, and I decided I would use the gift just one more time, to find out what was going on."

"What was it?"

"Oh, no, sugar, it's not my place to tell you that. It doesn't concern you, anyway, it's between me and your mom. But I broke my promise. I thought no one would ever know. I . . . found out the answer to a question, and I thought that would settle my mind. I thought then I could keep my peace.

"But in the end, even after I swore that I would keep it to myself, I couldn't. I'd used the gift and now it was like I had no choice but to pass along what I had learned. But that was a mistake, Clare. I had to tell, and in telling what I knew, I set into motion a series of happenings. . . . Well, I have had to suffer the consequences ever since. And I will until the day I die."

"But this other thing, whatever it was you found out—it wasn't your fault, right? All you did was tell someone."

Nana shook her head. "Sometimes knowing and telling is the worst thing you can do." Her voice wavered and she took a moment, dabbing at her forehead with the handkerchief she pulled from her pocket before speaking again. "If you dig deeper into this mess, there is no telling the terrible things you'll see. Amanda is gone and it is very likely that she will never come back. We just have to be realistic about it. The odds, in a disappearance like this—

well, I'm just saying that knowing things can hurt you. It could hurt her poor mother and that woman has suffered enough. Let it rest, Clare, angel. Let it go. It's for the best."

"But Nana—"

"You have to trust me on this. I'm old." Nana said it matter-of-factly. "I've lived through a lot and seen a lot, I've made my mistakes and I like to think I've learned from them. You let this go, now."

I couldn't promise that, but I nodded anyway.

"Now you remember what we talked about. You're being careful this week, right?"

"Yes, Nana."

"You're coming to the festival, aren't you? You and your friends come see me at the loggerhead booth, okay?"

"Sure," I promised, my heart sinking, knowing I was lying to her. There was no way I was dragging my friends over to see her and all her weird friends with their life-size photos of endangered turtles.

She gave my hand a final squeeze and got up from the table, going to the wall where a calendar hung on a nail, its image a photo of sea lions sunning themselves on rocks. "Now let me take a look . . . I think I've waited long enough for your mom to call me, so I'm just going to have to call her. I think I can probably guilt her into a dinner invitation, don't you?" She gave me a sly look and a wink, but I knew she was nervous about contacting my mom.

"Why don't you let me suggest it to her?" I said. "I'll work on her and then I'll call you. And Nana—" I hesitated, not sure how to apologize for ignoring her. "Um, I'll come visit more often," I finally said. "If that's okay."

"More than okay," Nana said. "When am I going to meet this boyfriend of yours? I know his uncle Arthur. He takes care of Peaches. Lovely man."

I felt myself blush. "Nana! He's—we're not—"

"I don't suppose I need to know what you are or aren't, Clare, it's just a dinner. Invite the boy, it'll take the pressure off me a little. What do you say?"

"I—I'll think about it."

"Can't ask for more than that. Now, get on home before Susie gets to worrying."

CHAPTER SEVENTEEN

As I coasted down the hill on my bicycle, stealing glances at the sun sinking low in the sky, I tried to convince myself that Nana was right, I should just stay out of it. I would get rid of the box of clothes today.

But when I got home, I found my mother sitting on the porch staring out over the ocean. Her face looked tired, the lines around her eyes and mouth more pronounced than usual.

"Are you feeling okay?" I asked, locking my bike to one of the posts that held up the porch.

"Fine," she said tightly. "Only, this came, after I thought we'd talked about it. I thought we'd come to an understanding."

She lifted a piece of paper off the table and held it out to me as though it were radioactive.

"Oh," I said after I scanned the print. It was the application to the Los Angeles Fashion Institute, the one I'd ordered from the website. "I, um, I wanted to see the application."

"Clare, you're only sixteen years old. You have two years left in high school. College applications aren't due for an entire year. And when that time comes, you'll have a lot more opportunities than just going to a two-year trade school."

I felt myself getting angry all over again. We'd had this conversation so many times before, and neither one of us could ever get the other to budge.

"This is what I want to do!" I said, louder than I intended. If my mom wanted to start a fight on our porch, then all the neighbors could damn well know about it. "I want to go into fashion. I always have. You *know* that. You see how hard I work. I do everything you ask me to, I have good grades and—"

"But that's exactly the point!" Bright pink spots stood out on my mother's cheeks. "You have *great* grades, Clare. You have the potential to do something meaningful. Go to a good school, take your time, study the humanities—"

"Why? So you can say I went to UCLA or Berkeley or somewhere you can brag about? And who are you going to impress, anyway, since you don't have any friends and you've even managed to drive your own mother away?"

I saw my mom's eyes go wide and I instantly regretted the words, but I was too upset to take them back. "You need to get a *life*, Mom. You can't live through me anymore. If you won't help me with design school, I'll pay for it myself. I'll work, I'll save, I don't care if it takes me ten years to get through the program, I *will* do it."

My mom's mouth dropped open and some of the anger faded into fear. And suddenly I realized that I was doing exactly the same thing my mother had done to Nana— threatening her with pushing her out of my life, just to get my way.

"Mom," I whispered, "I'm sorry, I didn't mean—"

"No." Her voice wavered, and she pushed away tears. "Don't."

Then she got up and went into the house, leaving me to stare out at the best view in town.

Alone.

• • •

In a few hours, we were being civil to each other. She didn't mention the application again, and neither did I. I volunteered to go and get takeout and Mom offered me the car without even being asked.

At the Chinese place we both liked, I was waiting for my order, reading a newspaper that someone had left on a chair, when Victoria came in with Jenna Liu and a middle-aged woman I assumed was her mother.

"Clare!" Victoria said, hugging me. "Mom, this is Clare Knight. You know, who moved back into the haunted house?"

"Oh, honey, don't call it that," Mrs. Abelson said, blushing.

"Welcome back to town, Clare. Are you getting settled in all right?"

"Yes, thank you." I'd gotten used to people's reactions, and was finding that it bothered me less as time went on. Eventually everyone would figure out that my mom and I weren't ghost hunters or cult members or whatever impression they'd all gotten of us. "We're still existing on takeout, but otherwise we're mostly moved in."

"I'll have to give your mother a call. See if she'd like to join my hiking group. Does she like to hike?"

"Uh, yes," I lied, making a note to suggest to my mom that she invest in a pair of hiking boots. Maybe this would be a way to get her out of the house.

Mrs. Abelson went to place their order while Victoria and Jenna stayed with me.

"Are you coming to Kane's serial killer party?" Victoria asked. "His folks are out of town."

"Hush, Vic," Jenna said. "If your mom hears that, she'll never let you go. Everyone's saying they're coming to my house," she added. "I live a few doors down so you can park there and walk over."

"You can dress as your favorite killer in history," Victoria said.

"Only the guys are doing that, though," Jenna said. "I think it's disgusting. And tacky."

"I'll think about it," I said.

"Listen, have you talked to Rachel today?" Victoria asked me. "I'm worried about her."

"Um, yeah, actually, I went to see her," I said, wondering how much to say. "She seemed a lot better today."

"Good. She really needs to tone it down before the elections," Jenna said. "I mean, *I'm* voting for her, but not everyone's as open-minded."

"What she means is not every Gold Key girl is willing to slum with the likes of me," Victoria said cheerfully.

"Sure, you can joke about it," Jenna said, rolling her eyes. "Your parents didn't grow up here so they're not on your case all the time."

"Was your mom a member too?" I asked her. It was impossible not to notice that most of the members belonged to Rachel's group, the most popular kids in school. The ones who set the trends, excelled in sports, had all the leadership positions. I could see where that would be important to a certain type of parent.

"Yeah, she's insane. I told her if she doesn't ease up on me I'm going to have a breakdown like Rachel did and end up hospitalized."

"What?" I blinked in surprise.

"She didn't tell you? Freshman year, she was gone for a couple of weeks. She was in this inpatient thing at the hospital. She had some sort of anxiety attack. I mean, she's all better now."

"Oh. That. Sure." It was weird, but as I kept finding out things Rachel had hidden from me, I found that I wanted to protect her almost as much as I wanted to ask her what the hell she was thinking. But I was damn sure going to find out what was going on. "Is she going to be at Kane's?"

"I'm sure she will," Victoria said. "Rachel never misses a party."

. . .

Mom and I ate in front of the television, and she fell asleep during a *CSI* rerun. But I hadn't been paying attention to the show. I'd been thinking about Rachel, and all her increasingly crazy behavior. Did she really think she was in danger? Or was she the one who was a danger herself? Did her breakdown freshman year signal some sort of ongoing mental instability? Was she *crazy*? Could she really be capable of hurting Amanda—over something as minor as membership in an exclusive club?

I checked on my mother. Still asleep, making a gentle sound on the exhale that wasn't quite a snore, full of weariness. I was still angry about what had happened earlier, but that wasn't an argument we could resolve in a day.

I left a note—"Went to Rachel's"—but I knew if Mom woke up she wasn't likely to check on me; she'd just go to bed.

Jenna had given me directions to Kane's house. I took my bike, and it was an uphill ride, as it was every time I went to visit the rich part of Winston. His house was well lit and there were cars parked all around the cul-de-sac, so I parked my bike behind a tall flowering arbor.

The front door was open so I went on in, recognizing

many of the kids who were standing around the living room drinking from red plastic cups. There had to be thirty kids in the living room and kitchen alone, and I could see that the back door was open, leading out to more people in the backyard standing around the pool. Someone had dragged a keg into the back and there was a table set up with bottles. It looked like a lot of people were already drunk.

I heard shouting from the yard, and people crowded the kitchen, trying to get out the back door to see what was going on. I let the crowd carry me to the back, keeping an eye out for Rachel. Everyone was standing around two guys on the grass. Great—another fight, except this didn't look like the usual joking-around brawling that the guys were always getting into on the beach.

It was semi-dark, the only light coming from the landscape lighting and party lights around the patio, so it took me a minute to figure out that the guy who was lunging and throwing drunken punches was Luke. He was wearing a sweatshirt I recognized, a dark smear of something along the sleeve.

"I'll say it again!" he yelled, swinging wildly. "I'll say anything I want!" The other guy blocked the hit with his forearm and stepped out of the way as Luke crashed down again onto the ground.

"Hey, hey, cut that shit out," someone said, pushing the standing fighter out of the way. He held up his hands and stepped back, and as the glow of a light hanging from a tree crossed his face, I recognized him.

Jack. It was Jack who'd managed to send Luke down

without even hitting him. Luke was crawling toward him, struggling to get up.

Jack said something quietly enough that I didn't hear it. A few paces away, Kane clapped a hand to his forehead. "My folks are going to kill me if anything happens."

"I'll go," Jack said, a little louder.

No one argued with him. They just stood aside so he could leave. He stalked toward the house and at the last minute I stepped out in front of him.

"Clare," he said, sounding surprised. "What are you doing here?"

"I was *invited*," I said. "What about you?"

"Ask your friends," he said bitterly, and pushed past me. "I'm sure they'll tell you. I'm nothing but trouble, remember? And they're all innocent."

"Jack, wait. Please."

But he didn't, and I could hear the front door slam behind him. I thought about following, but there were people watching, and I didn't want to start more rumors. Besides, I hadn't found Rachel yet.

"I'll find you!" Luke bellowed after Jack as he staggered to his feet. "You better run!"

It was clear to everyone that he'd lost the fight, but he kept yelling for a few minutes until Kane and some of the other guys dragged him off. Nothing had been damaged, at least; they'd been fighting in the middle of the lawn.

"Did you see all that?"

I turned, startled, to find Rachel standing next to me. She was wearing jeans and a sweater, neither of them tight or even particularly well-fitting. And she had barely any makeup on.

"Hey," I said.

"Hey yourself." She looked embarrassed. "You want to come sit by the hot tub with me? I got you a Coke."

She held up two cans that hadn't been opened yet. She didn't seem the least bit drunk, and I followed her around the corner of the house to a small landscaped hot tub at the end of the larger pool. No one else was there, and we rolled up our jeans and put our feet in the water.

"So, your boyfriend was defending your honor," Rachel said.

"What are you talking about?"

"Jack. Luke said something to him. Don't worry, everyone knows you turned him down, but the story he's telling is . . . uh, a little different."

"Wait. Let me get this straight. Luke's saying I—"

"Gave him something to remember," Rachel said, giving me a leer. "But he said it to the wrong guy. One minute they're over by the keg and the next minute Jack hit him so hard he rolled into the yard. Came up fighting, though, I'll give him that much. And Jack only took the one swing. After that he stood there and took it. Let Luke come after him, but he was drunk enough I don't think he did much damage."

"Oh, no," I said. Luke had clearly not been happy when I turned him down the other night, but it was hard for me to accept that he'd been talking about me . . . that way. I felt sick to my stomach just thinking about what people were hearing, people I barely knew.

But Jack had defended me. With his fists, without thinking. Without even hesitating.

I'm nothing but trouble, remember?

It was the same impulsive anger I'd seen in the truck, the same white-hot reaction that quickly cooled and gave way to reason. But a lot could happen quickly.

"Listen, I . . . want to apologize," Rachel said. "For, you know. Before. I haven't told you everything. I just—I want you to know it doesn't have anything to do with you. The thing is, Cee-Cee, sometimes I feel like you're the only person I can talk to. The only person who hasn't already judged me. I want to show you something."

She dug in her pocket and pulled out a folded piece of paper. She smoothed it out on her knee, and I could see it was a lined page from a spiral notebook. In block letters written with a Sharpie, it said, "YOU'RE NEXT."

"It was on my windshield when I came out of the yogurt shop the other day," she said quietly. "Right on Beach in the middle of the afternoon. I think Mr. Granger put it there."

"How can you say that, Rachel? It could be anyone." I picked up the paper, turning it over; the back side was blank. "It could be kids playing a joke."

"No. Listen. What if he did it? What if the thing with Dillon was like an accident? I mean, everyone's seen Mr. Granger get completely out of control. He could have hit Dillon too hard, once too often. Completely without meaning to. And then he'd have to get rid of the body, right? It could have been him that put it over the cliff. He could have thrown the bike over too, and then called from the truck stop. Because he would have been out of his mind with grief, right, and he'd want them to find the body so Dillon could be properly buried and all. But the whole time he couldn't let them know what happened or he'd go to jail."

"Rachel, that's—that's insane." But I was remembering the way Mr. Granger looked, the expression on his face as he looked out over the crowd yesterday. Was he capable of something so cold? "Besides, why would he kill Amanda?"

Rachel shook her head. "I don't know. Maybe it isn't even related. Or maybe she figured it out, so he had to get rid of her. Or maybe it set off something in him, and he can't stop. . . ."

"That doesn't make any sense at all."

"Well, what about this?" she said, taking the piece of paper back from me and holding it up. "This doesn't make a lot of sense either, but it was there. Under my windshield."

"It could have been something completely different. It might have had nothing to do with those murders. It could have been anything," I said, thinking it could have even been Rachel who wrote the note, if she was as unbalanced as I was beginning to think. Maybe it was even an attempt to get attention. Maybe she was on the verge of another breakdown.

"Okay," Rachel said in a small voice, folding the note back up and putting it in her pocket. "Just, if I wind up dead, maybe you could tell the police to check out the Grangers, okay?"

CHAPTER EIGHTEEN

AN HOUR LATER I WAS HOME. Mom had gotten up from the couch at some point and gone to bed, probably never noticing I was gone. I got a glass of water from the kitchen, sat down in front of my computer, and Googled Mr. Granger.

Everything Rachel had said about him was true. Not only had he been barred from attending any game in the local league, the man he hit had filed suit against him. Later, when Dillon died, the charges were dropped.

So he was every bit as violent as Rachel had suggested. Still, it was a stretch from hitting an adult at a baseball game to killing his own son.

My phone chimed to signal a new text.

ARE U UP?

Jack. My breath caught—he was the last person I expected to hear from.

As soon as I typed YES I regretted it. The last time I'd

seen him, earlier tonight, he'd just hit someone so hard he was crawling on the ground. And oh, yeah, he refused to stop and talk to me—there was that, too. Why should I respond to him now?

Maybe because of the electric thrill I felt whenever I thought about him. Maybe because, among everyone who was anyone gathered at Kane's house tonight, there was still no other guy I was interested in.

And I wanted to talk to someone. Needed to, really, after all the things that had happened today.

I kept going through the possibilities—someone had killed both Dillon and Amanda; or there were two different killers at work; or Amanda wasn't dead at all, but either being held captive somewhere, or she'd run away for reasons of her own. As bad as Jack made her home life sound, though, it didn't seem like enough to make her leave, especially since she had been happy at school.

I couldn't shake the disturbing feeling that Amanda was no longer alive but wasn't at peace: she wanted justice and she was using me to get it, using my gift to talk to me through her clothes. And everyone else in Winston, with the exception of Mom and Nana—Rachel, Jack, the Grangers, Mrs. Stavros—seemed like they were hiding things or not telling the truth.

It had gotten chilly, even with Lincoln's old sweatshirt zipped up to my neck. I wrapped my arms around my bare legs and watched my screen saver change images. It was too much to sort out right now.

My phone buzzed and I almost dropped it.

CN I COME OVER

I felt a surge of excitement and . . . something else. Anticipation. Fear. Uncertainty. I wanted to talk about what was happening to me, but what was I doing considering involving Jack, someone I barely knew? I'd been so careful with my gift. None of my teachers knew. Not my dad, my friends from Blake. No one but Mom and Nana.

But I didn't have to tell him everything. We could just talk. . . .

While I was staring at the screen a second text came in.

NEED 2 TALK

That sealed it for me—Jack had barely spoken more than a sentence at a time the whole time I had known him. Maybe this was my chance to find out something about him. I typed quickly.

GIVE ME 10

I put the phone back in my pocket, my hands shaking. Adrenaline, fear, cold . . . It didn't matter. I quickly combed my hair and washed my face and exchanged Lincoln's sweatshirt for a sweater decorated with sequins at the neck and sleeves. Then I went out on the porch to wait, shivering as I watched clouds float across the moon, narrow wispy ones that barely dimmed its yellow glow.

I heard the engine from a block away, a powerful, low

humming sound. A moment later Jack pulled up in front of the house, leaning across to crank down the window.

"Want to go for a ride?" he called softly.

I got in the truck. Jack didn't look at me as he pulled away from the curb, driving slowly uphill.

"There's a place I know," he said.

So much for my hopes he'd have a lot to say.

I thought I knew every road in town, but it turned out there was a little gravel alley behind where San Benito Road ended at Third Street. Except it wasn't really an alley at all, but a winding road that went up and around the rocky slope that led to Nana's street. Instead of joining up with Ridge Avenue, it took a jog at a rock outcropping—my heart caught in my throat when I looked out the window over the steep drop as Jack took the turn—and continued up the hill, the road turning into a pair of rutted tracks surrounded by overgrown bramble.

"What is this?"

"Fire road," Jack said. "Dad used to bring me up here when . . ."

His voice faded and for a moment I thought he wasn't going to finish the thought. And then he spoke softly, a hint of humor in his voice. "Dad always said that some rules deserve to be broken—but if you didn't know which then you weren't qualified to break any."

I smiled in the dark despite myself. "So, you know the difference?"

"Took me a while, and I made a few mistakes, but yeah . . . I think I do."

The bumpy road flattened out and suddenly, spread out below us, was the entire town of Winston, a million sparkling lights with the serene black ocean beyond reflecting the yellow moon on its surface. "Oh . . . wow," I said, unable to come up with anything better.

Jack cut the engine, pulling the truck over so that the view from the windshield was straight ahead. "So, look," he said. "About Luke."

"Yeah, what was that?" I asked. "Do you just go around taking swings at everyone who pisses you off?"

Jack glared at me. If I was hoping for an apology, it looked like I wasn't going to get one. "Just the ones who call you a slut."

I blinked. Not what I had expected, and I was hit hard by the unfairness of it. "But I never—"

"Not my business what you did or didn't do with Herrera," Jack said grimly.

I still wanted to explain that nothing had happened with Luke, but I could see that Jack wasn't going to let me tell him the story. "Well—then why did you hit him?"

"Don't know."

That brought the conversation to a halt. And after a few minutes, Jack sighed.

"Okay, yeah, I know why. I didn't like it. I wanted to make sure he stopped saying it. So I hit him."

"You can't just settle every disagreement by hitting people," I said.

"Yeah, I got that. Thanks. That's why I only hit him

once. That's why I stood there and let him try to hit me until he got tired. Fucking idiot."

I couldn't help smiling to myself. "I thought you and Luke got suspended together in middle school."

"This is how guys settle things, Clare. Real guys, anyway."

"Real" guys, as opposed to Earl-Dobby-wearing rich kids from Grover Hill, I figured. Well, if I was Jack, I might have some resentment stored up too.

"Do you always try the violent way first?"

It wasn't the way I meant for it to come out, but suddenly the air between us was charged with tension. I seemed to have a way of always saying the wrong thing around Jack, always provoking him.

"Look, Clare, either you like me or you don't. I'm here. I came for you. I want you. Not the girl you think you have to be to fit into that crowd. But the girl I saw the other day"—he reached across the seat and touched my hair, pushing it away from my eyes—"with that stupid blue feather in her hair. The girl who looked like she could tell the world to go to hell."

I froze, his touch taking my breath from me. "I do," I whispered. *Like you. Want you.* But I couldn't get any more words out.

We met in the middle, somehow, of the seat. I don't remember moving toward him but the next second his hands were in my hair and my arms were wrapped around him, and his lips found mine and he kissed me like last time, except more. More of everything, and I was out of breath and I didn't care and I was so glad this truck was old enough to have a bench seat and that Jack knew where the fire road was and that we'd come back to Winston. Glad for all of it, even if it was just for a while, and I could forget all the rest and just be there with him.

After a while, a long while, he pulled me close against him and we sat in silence, looking at the view. I could make out our street far below—the Logans strung red, white, and blue lights around their porch for the Fourth of July—and the bright lights of the town. I thought I could see the Shuckster's parking lot, and the outdoor seating of the restaurants that lined the water, sparkling with candles. Out in the bay the lights of a few boats bobbed and floated.

"It's beautiful," I said after a while. "Do you bring all your girlfriends here?"

"Are you my girlfriend?"

"Uh, well . . ." I turned my face against his shirt. The fabric was soft, thick and well-washed. His warmth was irresistible.

"A few things you should know. This won't work if you have allergies, for starters. At least to animals. And you have to be able to put up with me reeking."

"You don't smell too bad," I murmured. That was actually an understatement—Jack smelled great, like soap and something spicy and well-worn, and really masculine. Leather or tobacco or something.

"Earlier tonight I smelled like cat urine and dog vomit."

"I don't have allergies," I said, smiling. "To answer your question."

Jack played with the hair at the back of my head, twisting it around his fingers and then releasing it. It would be so easy to let the evening sweep me along, to forget about what had happened earlier. To try to ignore my fears and have just one night with nothing on my mind but being here with Jack, under the stars, and falling . . . falling hard for him.

But I kept thinking about Mrs. Stavros, the Grangers; about Rachel and Amanda and Dillon. About touching the denim jacket, about trying to understand my role in everything that had happened. All of it. I needed to talk about it, to tell someone.

"Hey," Jack said, touching my face lightly. "You okay?"

I blushed in the dark, because he had read me so easily. I might be making my biggest mistake yet, but at some point I had to trust someone. And so I started talking.

I didn't mean to tell him everything. Not at first. I started with the argument with my mom, with how hard it was to know what I was meant to do with my life and having her disagree so completely. But from there it was an easy jump to the move here and trying to fit in, making friends, and holding back. And he listened. Jack really listened, staying quiet much of the time, asking a question once in a while.

Before I knew it I'd told him about finding out Rachel had been keeping things from me, my confusion about our friendship.

"What kind of things?" Jack asked. He was stroking my hair, pushing it behind my ears with his strong fingers. It felt so good. And so . . . safe.

Safe enough that I was walking along the edge of trusting him with things I'd never trusted anyone with.

But it involved him, too. His own life had been dramatically affected by Amanda's disappearance. He'd dealt with his own pain and loss, and he'd hit rock bottom before he recovered.

"I . . . don't know how to talk about it," I said carefully. "It's about Amanda. About what happened to her."

There was a long pause, his fingers still in my hair. I could feel his breathing, slow and sure, his chest rising and falling gently against my cheek.

"All right. I'm listening."

I'd expected him to pull back. I had been ready to stop, to change the subject, to accept that we wouldn't be able to get around this obstacle in our relationship. And yet I couldn't *not* say it, either. Being with Jack wasn't like being with any of the other boys I had dated; I felt like we connected in a way that no one else had ever come close to. If we were going to be together I wanted to be completely honest with him. Even about the things that were hard.

Even about the things that were secret.

And if, after hearing what I had to say, he turned away from me, I'd deal with it then. Maybe he'd think I was crazy. Maybe he wouldn't ever speak to me again. But at least I would have tried. I was so tired of watching what I said, what I revealed about myself. I was tired of being ashamed of what I could do, of thinking of my gift as a curse. I felt safe when I was with Jack, even though lots of people would say that was crazy, given his record; I felt as though he already saw into me, felt what I felt and didn't judge me for it. And I wanted to take it farther. Wanted to show him more. For once, I wanted to stop hiding, to reveal both what I could do and who I really was.

I took a deep breath. "I . . . There's this thing I can do."

But that didn't feel right. How could I explain something it had taken years for me to understand? And even now I was still learning. I burrowed deeper against his soft, warm shirt and Jack wrapped his arms around me, holding me closer. I tried again.

"A week or two ago, when I first went to the flea market . . ."

Once I got going, the words just flowed, faster and faster, until I was interrupting myself, trying to express how it had felt to hold the jacket in my hands the first time, what it was like to look into Mrs. Stavros's cloudy eyes and see her pain, how afraid I'd been when Mr. Granger looked at me. How betrayed I felt knowing Rachel had lied to me. All of it. I didn't pull away from Jack's chest, and he didn't say anything. But he never stopped holding me and he never interrupted, and when I'd reached the end, when I'd told him everything, he was silent for a while longer. His hands rubbed my back and he kissed my hair, and then he touched his fingers gently to my chin, tipping up my head so I was looking at him.

"You're not crazy, Clare," he finally said. "I'm not sure exactly what you are. But crazy's not the word for it."

I held my breath, sure he was going to tell me that he

had to go, that he wished me luck but he couldn't get involved with something like this.

But he didn't.

Inside the truck, lit by starlight and warm with our own
body heat, Jack didn't let go.

"Where's the jacket now?" he said suddenly. I thought I
detected a sense of urgency in his voice, and a tiny alarm
sounded, deep in the recesses of my mind. Why was he
asking? For what possible reason would he need to know,
unless the jacket was connected in some way . . . to him?

No, that was insane. I'd *know*. I'd know if he wasn't who
he said he was. If I couldn't believe that, then I couldn't
believe anything at all. "It's safe," I said, thinking, *That's all
you need to know. Please don't ask me to tell you any more. Don't
make me doubt you.*

He kissed me on the lips, so soft I almost didn't feel it.
"So what do we do now?"

• • •

Jack didn't drive very fast down the fire road, the truck
bouncing on the rutted dirt, but he made record time back
to our neighborhood. Even so, it was very late, and when
we pulled up in front of my house, I saw that all the lights
were on inside.

Jack had said almost nothing on the way home, each of
us lost in our own thoughts. I was working really hard to
keep my doubts at bay, and Jack . . . Well, who knew what
went on in his mind?

"Don't get out, I'm good," I said, figuring he hadn't been planning to anyway. "Thank you so much. For, you know. Everything." I opened the door, trying to keep things from being awkward, but I succeeded only in making everything feel more awkward, especially when he leaned across the seat and put his hand out to prevent me from shutting the door.

"Nothing to thank me for."

Yeah, I got that. I was just making conversation. "Are you going to the festival Wednesday?"

"Not sure."

Of course he wasn't sure. That was the thing about Jack, he was so hard to pin down. "Well, okay, I'll probably be there, so if you go I might—"

"Clare," he said, cutting me off. "Call me. Or I'll call you. This doesn't have to be hard."

And with that, he pulled the door shut before I could think of anything to say in response. I listened to the sound of the truck disappearing slowly down the street as I walked up our steps and let myself in the front door.

The silence lasted only a fraction of a second.

"Clare!"

My mother came running from the living room, almost tripping over the soft brown afghan that she liked to drape over herself while watching television. Her face was swollen and her hair had come halfway out of its ponytail and was falling crazily into her face. She'd been crying, I realized with a shock.

"Mom, I'm so sorry, I know it's late—"

She wrapped me into a fierce hug, her arms so tight around me I could barely breathe. "Oh my God, you have no idea how worried I've been—"

"I know, I know."

"No. You *don't* know."

Her voice was ragged, and I looked at her sharply, noticing that the line between her eyebrows was etched with worry, that there were dark smudges under her eyes.

"Mom, I—"

"Clare, every night on the news they've been talking about what happened to those kids, about how they never caught the killer. I can't lose you. I just can't."

"Mom, nothing's going to happen to me, okay? I'm careful. I don't—"

"You don't *nothing*. You don't know. You're a child. I'm— I've seen more than you have. People can be ugly. They can be *bad*."

"You think I don't know that? I'm *not* a child anymore! Not like that, anyway. Did you think you could protect me just by telling me to stop reading clothes?"

"What is that supposed to mean?" Her gaze snapped up at me, and I could see the fear as well as the anger in her expression.

"You can't do it, so it scares you. That's why you made Nana stop. That's why you made me stop." I was so angry, I couldn't keep from blurting it out. "But guess what—it's not that simple. Maybe we all can't just turn it off."

Mom drew in her breath sharply, her eyebrows lowering

angrily. "What did Nana tell you? She made a *promise* to me—"

"Yeah, for *you*. She did it for you, Mom! Do you have any idea how hard it is not to use the gift?"

Mom rolled her eyes. *"The gift,"* she repeated. "I suppose you got that from Nana too. How anyone could consider it a gift—it's a curse, Clare, something I've wished a million times that she hadn't passed along to you. I was spared, and I thought you would be too, but I guess she was right all along. Nana always said it was in our blood. I just never believed her. I never wanted to believe her."

"You made *both* of us stop," I whispered so angrily I could barely keep my voice steady. "First her, and then me. She wouldn't tell me what it was, just that she made some mistake and you threatened never to speak to her again if she ever used the gift. Is that what you're going to do to me too? Cut me off completely? Throw me out?"

"Oh my God, no, Clare," my mother said, seeming to be genuinely horrified. "I would never do that, you have to believe—"

"Then how could you do it to *her*?"

"You don't understand. That was different. She—she used it to hurt me."

My mouth fell open. "Nana? Nana wanted to *hurt* you? I don't believe you. You should see how she looks when she talks about you. It's killing her, you have to—"

"You don't know."

"So tell me!"

Both of us were yelling, our voices echoing around our small living room. I hadn't realized I was crying, but hot tears fell on my collarbone and Mom clutched the blanket so tightly that her knuckles were white.

"You want to know? Okay, maybe it's time. Maybe it's time you understand exactly what this so-called *gift* of yours can do. How it can destroy people. And families. I was still in high school when your grandmother promised she'd never use the gift again, but she broke her promise. When you were ten."

The year we moved.

The year Dad left us.

"Oh, Clare . . . I'd always planned to tell you someday, but I just wanted you to be ready. To be a little older, so that you—"

"I'm old enough *now*."

My mother sighed, rubbing her fingers along her temples. "We'd gone over to her house for a barbecue. Some of the neighbors were over. Your father and a couple of the other men were helping fix a trellis and you and I were helping in the kitchen . . . Anyway, your father got dirty and your grandmother gave him an old T-shirt to wear, promising to wash his shirt. I didn't think anything of it. But the next week when she brought it back to me, all clean and folded . . ."

I almost asked her to stop. Because I knew, deep down, what was coming.

"She told me she couldn't help it." Mom's voice dropped to a whisper. "She said when she touched it she felt . . . all your father's emotions . . . his discontent, how trapped he felt, how—how he wanted to escape, to be with . . . *her,* with Renee. . . . She said I needed to know, so I could 'make decisions.' She meant so I could leave him, of course."

"Oh, Mom . . ." My anger drained away instantly. My dad. Of course it had to do with my dad. The man who'd stuck around just long enough to make sure that when he left, he'd rip big enough holes to ruin both our lives. "I'm so sorry."

I'd never known the exact story about Dad and Renee and how they ended up together. She'd been his assistant, that was all I knew. Mom had told me they'd started dating after the divorce, but he'd moved in with Renee shortly after he left us. And a few months after that he'd taken a job in Sacramento, where they bought a house together.

But I'd never come out and asked. I guess I hadn't really wanted to know.

"*Sorry.*" Mom laughed, a short, bitter sound. "Not as sorry as I was. After my mother told me I had no choice but to confront my husband about the affair he was having. So I did. And he didn't even try to deny it. He never even asked me how I knew—that was how little he cared. He was gone a few days later."

"But Mom—if he was that unhappy, he would have left anyway—"

"Not like *that!*" Now my mother was crying in earnest. "Not with me . . . humiliated . . . Straight into the arms of his *assistant,* of all the women in the world, that's such a cliché, Clare, you don't even understand."

But I did understand.

I knew exactly how my mother felt: abandoned, tossed aside, unwanted. It was exactly how Dad had made me feel, too. But somehow, she didn't see that we had that in common. In her mind, she was the only one who'd suffered from what he'd done.

"You can't blame this on Nana," I said. "All she did was tell you what he was already doing."

"Don't you get it, Clare? If your grandmother had kept it to herself—if she'd never gone looking into things that didn't concern her—that affair would have burned itself out. Your father would have gotten it out of his system and we would have had some dignity."

"Are you *kidding* me? Are we talking about the same guy? My dad, Joe Knight? The one who sent me a birthday card two months late? Oh, yeah, all he needed was a little time, right? And he would have been husband and father of the fucking *year*."

"*Clare!*"

I had never talked to her like that before, but I wasn't going to stop until I was through. "You put all this on Nana," I said shakily, barely able to control my fury. "But it was never about her. It was *Dad's* fault, not hers. You made us move, you turned your back on her . . . you even made it about *me*. Do you have any idea how— I thought I was a *freak*, Mom. All because you made the things I could do seem shameful. I've tried so hard to do what you wanted, to make you happy, but I'm not going to anymore."

"Clare . . ."

"*No.*" I jerked away from her. "No. I'm going to my room. I want to be by myself. You already ruined Nana's life, I'm not going to let you ruin mine too. I am who I am, Mom, and you need to decide if you can love me this way or not. Or it won't matter what else happens. You can't make me safe by pretending I'm someone I'm not."

I didn't turn around as I ran for my room, slamming the door, but I could hear her sobbing even after I got into my bed and pulled the covers up over my head.

CHAPTER NINETEEN

I WOKE AROUND NINE THE NEXT morning, groggy and disoriented. I lay in bed for a while thinking about Jack and Rachel and Amanda and Dillon, about the secrets simmering below the surface of the town as they prepared for tomorrow's festival.

When I finally got up, Mom was gone, but the house smelled amazing. Wandering into the kitchen, I found a German apple pancake sitting on the stove, still warm. It was perfect, puffy and sprinkled with powdered sugar. It broke my heart, thinking of my mom rushing to make it for me before she went to work.

I knew that getting up early to bake was a kind of apology. I owed her an apology too, but I wasn't sure where to start. I was still angry, but everything was muddy now, confusing and unclear. Yes, it was wrong of my mother to shift the blame to Nana for what my father did, but she was only human . . . heartbroken, left with a child to raise by herself, needing to make a living for us both.

It wasn't until I'd poured myself a glass of juice that I noticed my mother had left something else for me. Neatly folded next to the coffee maker was a soft green shirt, with a note on top in my mother's careful handwriting.

Clare—I wore this when I was pregnant with you. Your grandmother did the embroidery. I could never bear to give it away.

Love, Mom

I unfolded the shirt. It was a simple style, with an Empire waistline gathered with tiny pin tucks. The neckline had been embellished with a trailing design of flowers and leaves in silk embroidery floss a shade lighter than the cotton fabric. The handwork was beautiful, French knots dotting the chain-stitch flowers, leaves in satin stitch. Nana had shown me how to do a few of these stitches when I was little, but my attempts had always been a mess.

I held the shirt up to my cheek. There was a faint spicy scent, as if it had been stored in a drawer with sachets.

I felt a wave of sadness for my mom. She had never been comfortable showing her emotions. Even now, when I knew she had to be lonely, she never talked about it. The stack of books on her nightstand grew, and she distracted herself with more work, but she needed friends.

I thought of Mrs. Stavros, alone with her grief and her drinking.

And I wondered: Could they help each other? Could my mother help her old friend move forward with her life?

I knew Mrs. Stavros would never get over the loss of her daughter, but maybe she could turn herself around enough to stop hiding in her own house, have some friends, maybe work. If her ex-husband was as rich as everyone said, she probably didn't need the money, but if she didn't do something she was going to waste away in her mansion.

Maybe getting back into her old life would be a good start for my mom. I could talk to Mrs. Stavros, maybe invite her over for coffee, tell my mom she was coming only when it was too late for her to cancel.

The day stretched out long and empty in front of me. I needed to call Rachel but I didn't have the energy for that yet. And besides, she was busy getting ready to leave town later in the afternoon. With her gone, that would be one less person I needed to worry about tomorrow, on the actual anniversary.

The whole town was holding its breath, trying to get through the next forty-eight hours. The crazy thing was, there were no guarantees; even if nothing bad happened tomorrow, what about the day after that? And the one after that?

There was no end date on trying to discover what had happened to Amanda, and who had killed Dillon. Walking around Winston, you got the feeling that if we all got through this week, there would be this huge sigh of relief and everyone would be able to pretend nothing bad had ever happened. The tourists would come back. The businesses would start earning profits again. Alone in their houses, the grieving parents would continue to mourn the children they had lost, but out in the streets of town Mrs. Granger would smile and greet people and move ahead with her life. Maybe, in time, her husband and Mrs. Stavros would too.

The only loose thread in this whole plan was me. I had the visions, the jacket, the need to find out what happened. Now, maybe, I had an ally. But if last night I had felt like I could trust Jack completely, in the bright light of morning common sense returned. I wanted to see Jack, have him beside me as I hunted down the truth. But I was going to take one precaution . . . just in case I was making a huge mistake with him.

I got the plastic bag from my backpack, trying not to look at its contents. It was cool and squishy in my hands as I went down into the cellar. Most houses in Winston didn't have basements, but the dress shop had been built over a dirt cellar used for storage long ago. When my parents renovated, they'd had some foundation repairs made but left the cellar alone. I remembered seeing spider nests, old broken glass, and bits of paper and ancient trash down there. We'd never used it for storage because of the damp and dirt, but long ago my ancestors had, and there were niches and decaying wooden shelves lining the walls.

The single bulb overhead did little to illuminate the space, and the dust made me sneeze, but I took my time, considering and discarding half a dozen spaces before I found a relatively sturdy shelf in one corner. It had been constructed of raw lumber many decades ago, and as I brushed dust off the boards with my sleeve, I saw that something had been written on the wood.

I squinted in the near darkness. A single word had been written in a childish hand: "Josie." My great-great-grandmother. Alma's daughter, raised by her mother's sister, who went on to work in the shop upstairs, who passed her mother's dark gift on to her own daughter and, many years later, to me.

I wondered what she had kept down here. Incomplete projects, maybe, or patterns. Yard goods or a stash of fabrics she'd collected. Or maybe this was where she kept her private things—journals and treasures, love letters and hopes for the future. Whatever she'd stored here, it was long gone.

I touched the wood, wondering if I'd be able to feel the connection across time. But all I felt was the dirty, splintering board. I slid the plastic bag far back on the shelf—and my fingertips brushed against something.

My heartbeat quickened as I closed my fingers around a small round object and brought it into the light. A button. I rubbed it on my shirt to get rid of the layers of grime, and saw that it was beautiful, made of shimmering mother-of-pearl and edged in scalloped silver.

Turning it this way and that in the light of the bare bulb, I was certain that this small treasure had belonged to my great-grandmother. I felt like Josie had left it there just for me to find, as reassurance that everything would be all right, that I could trust my gift.

I slipped the button into my pocket, feeling like I had found the thing I didn't know I was looking for.

Half an hour later I was showered and out the door, pedaling across town to the Stavros house, the button tucked in the pocket of my shorts. I liked knowing it was there, especially since I wasn't entirely sure what I was doing. I felt like I was trying to arrange a playdate for my mom, like somewhere along the line the tables had gotten turned and we'd switched roles. But I was trying to help Mrs. Stavros, too. I had run out of ideas for trying to figure out Amanda's disappearance, but maybe coming at it from a new angle would spark something.

It probably made more sense to start with my mom, but that was going to be a tough sell. Mom could be really stubborn, and if she knew I was trying to push her into a friendship, she'd probably resist. But once they were in the same room . . . well, wasn't there a chance that something would spark?

As I coasted onto Elderberry Circle, my ankles getting sprayed by the sprinklers as I rode past the beautiful lawns, I felt hopeful that this would help me move on too. Dillon's death, Amanda's disappearance, they were just sad statistics, lives ended too early, leaving heartbreak and pain behind. But nothing I did now would change that.

Walking up the Stavroses' drive, I noticed a car I knew parked next to the dark red Acura that had been there the day before: a sleek blue Mercedes with a crystal charm hanging from the rearview mirror.

Rachel's mom's car.

I'd ridden in it half a dozen times when she took us out for dinner or to go shopping. She didn't like to ride in Rachel's car because she said it messed up her hair.

What was she doing here? Rachel had never mentioned her mom and Mrs. Stavros being in touch. Had they kept their friendship up without Rachel knowing? Or was Mrs. Slade just checking in on an old friend, someone she knew was struggling, maybe coming over to talk and have coffee?

If she hadn't seen Mrs. Stavros in a while, though, she was in for a shock.

While I was standing there trying to figure out what to do, the front door flew open so forcefully it bounced against the wooden bench on the front porch, and Mrs. Slade backed out, tripping on one of her pink wedge-heeled sandals and grabbing the bench to steady herself.

"Get out, get *out*." Mrs. Stavros was standing in the door sobbing, her hair even more of a mess than it had been yesterday. Her face was shiny with tears and her bangs were stuck to her forehead, mascara smudged under her eyes.

"Heaven, I'm telling you, you've put us all at risk." Mrs. Slade looked angry, and she jammed her foot in the door so Mrs. Stavros couldn't pull it shut. "I'm going to go now, but I'm coming back when you're sober, and we're going to figure out a *plan*. Just promise me you won't talk to anyone else."

"We're going to figure out a plan," Mrs. Stavros mimicked, her face twisted as she echoed Mrs. Slade's words. "You always had to tell everyone else what to do, Brenda. But

you're not the one who lost a daughter. So you don't get to push me around anymore."

"Heaven, you know how terrible we all feel about that, how much we miss Amanda—"

"Right, I know, but you still get to go home to Rachel and Adrienne and Cal. The perfect little family. What do I have? Nothing. *Nothing.* And it was every bit as much Rachel's fault as Amanda's. What's fair about that? Huh?"

She swayed on her feet, blinking, trying to focus on Mrs. Slade, who looked like she was about to jump out of her skin. "Quiet," she hissed. "Do you want the whole neighborhood to hear?"

"But I said—"

"I am very sorry about Amanda, and I always will be, you know that, Heaven, but it was *not* the same. Amanda was driving. Not Rachel. And I will not let you drag her down with you, I swear to you—"

"I'll talk to whoever I want," Mrs. Stavros said, almost to herself. "You can't make me stop."

I backed down the driveway as carefully as I could, glad I'd worn my rubber-soled Converse sneakers. I couldn't let them see me. I could still hear the sound of Mrs. Stavros's crying and Mrs. Slade's tense, fast talking as I coasted down the circle.

My head was full of questions, the shock of what I'd overheard numbing my senses. I was dimly aware of cars, lawn mowers, kids yelling in the park, but it wasn't until I almost ran into a car door that I realized that if I didn't calm down, I was going to get into an accident. I turned onto another residential street, pedaling slowly and taking the long way down the hill, crisscrossing the neighborhood and avoiding the main road.

Mrs. Slade was angry that Mrs. Stavros had been talking to someone—and it didn't take a genius to guess who she meant. *Me.* Mrs. Slade had somehow found out that I'd visited Mrs. Stavros, and she wasn't the least bit happy about it.

Amanda was driving. . . .

It was every bit as much Rachel's fault as Amanda's. . . .

I felt the beginnings of a headache. I'd reached the bottom of Lycester Court, where I could turn right toward my house or left across town to Rachel's. I'd steered to the left even before I was aware of deciding.

• • •

"So you're my self-appointed bodyguard now?"

Rachel was digging into her single scoop of strawberry ice cream from the Frosty Top. She seemed mostly back to normal, if exhausted; nearly all traces of the instability in the last few days were gone.

I was probably the only person in town who didn't think much of the Frosty Top's twenty flavors, but that was because I wasn't all that into ice cream, period. My thing was the kettle corn they sold down by the pier, hot and salty and sweet and fresh out of the warmer. But I was so desperate to get Rachel out of the house that I told her we could go to Frosty Top and I'd even pay. Now we were sitting out on the pier having ice cream for lunch, ignoring the tourists walking back and forth who irritated the guys who were there to fish. We always sat in this one place where the fishing was supposed to be bad, and since no one ever dumped bait here, the gulls didn't tend to mess it up as much.

I pushed my Gummi bears around in my melting vanilla yogurt, not really feeling like eating.

"Rachel . . . I need to ask you something."

"Okay," she said, wiggling her bare toes and admiring her pedicure.

"I just wondered . . ." I hesitated, knowing I was about to risk the one good friendship I had here in Winston. I took a deep breath, carefully setting my yogurt cup down on the splintery pier. "Where were you the night Dillon Granger died?" I asked quietly.

There was a long pause, and when Rachel spoke again her voice was strange—thin and hollow. "What are you talking about, Clare?"

The inside of the car. The phone in my hand. The jolt, the bump, the pain.

"When someone threw him off the cliff. When they made that nine-one-one call from the truck stop. I just wondered where you were."

"I don't know, Clare, it was a long time ago, I guess I was probably home watching TV or something, or, I don't know, at a movie or the mall or—"

I knew she was lying, knew it from the way she still wouldn't look at me and was talking too fast, the words tripping over each other. And it hurt to know she was lying to me—but then again, I'd kept a secret from her, too. One I still couldn't tell.

"Stop," I said, very softly. "Stop a minute. Please?"

She did, and her eyes darted toward me, long enough for me to see that she was scared.

"I know Amanda was driving," I said carefully. And I'd known it for a while now, deep down inside, though it took seeing Mrs. Slade and Mrs. Stavros arguing to understand what it meant. "I know that she was texting. That she never meant to hurt him. She just looked away from the road for a second and that was all it took. Her car ran off the road onto the shoulder and she ran into Dillon's bike, just hard enough to push him over, and the rail was broken. That wasn't her fault. I know it wasn't."

Rachel was staring right at me now, the color draining from her face. Her lips parted slightly, and she said something like "Oh," the ice cream falling from her fingers and bouncing off the rocks lining the pier right into the water. Seawater filled the cup, mixing with the pink ice cream as tiny narrow fish darted instantly to the surface to check it out.

"What I think must have happened was that Amanda called her mom, and Mrs. Stavros told her to go home. Then she called it in. She picked the truck stop because she knew a call from a pay phone couldn't be traced to her, and she got lucky, no one saw her. That was taking a chance but I guess Mrs. Stavros felt like she had to. That she had no other choice. Because Amanda was her daughter."

Rachel had gone ghostly pale, her lower lip trembling.

I wanted to hug her, wanted to stop this terrible story, to say it didn't matter. But her reaction confirmed my fears. Whatever had happened . . .

It was every bit as much Rachel's fault as Amanda's.

Rachel knew something. And I was giving her one more chance to tell me.

"Who told you?" she finally said, in a whisper so soft the wind and the shouts of the tourists threatened to drown her out.

"No one told me, Rachel, I just . . . I just found out. Okay? I won't tell anyone, I swear it." *But if you don't, that damn jacket will never let me alone. You understand, don't you, that I'm taking orders from a couple of yards of cotton denim and a handful of tin buttons. Crazy—who, me? Just because every time I touch it I think it's trying to drag me down with it?* Sure. Rachel would understand.

She bit her bottom lip, a gesture I'd only seen her make once or twice before, one that made her suddenly seem so much younger. Her blond hair blew around her face, and I was so close I could count her freckles.

"I haven't told anyone," she said softly, and her hand inched across the warm wood. I laced my fingers through hers and she squeezed hard. She wasn't just afraid, I realized with a start, she was *terrified.*

"I—I mean what I said. I won't let anything bad happen to you, Rachel. I won't tell, whatever it is."

"She wanted to see Jack that night," she said, wiping her eyes with the sleeve of her free hand. "I didn't want to do it. I was tired of being her excuse. She had . . . everything."

"Were you," I started, trying to figure out how to ask it. Then I decided to just be direct. "You were frustrated with her, right? Did you feel taken advantage of?"

"Yes," Rachel said quietly. "I felt like everything was so easy for her. Like she didn't ever have to work for it."

"Is that why you took her necklace?"

Rachel froze, then stared at me with wide eyes. "How did you know about that?"

"Listen, Rachel, I can't tell you, I just—"

"It was that time you slept over, right? When you borrowed my earrings? Did you see it then?"

I remembered the night she was talking about. We'd been getting ready to go to the beach for the first time since I moved back, and I had on these silver skull earrings that had little fake ruby eyes. I thought they were adorable but Rachel said they sent the wrong message. She told me to look through her jewelry box and pick something, any-thing, else. I did it, mostly because I was feeling so insecure that first time. I'd borrowed a pair of silver hoops. But I hadn't noticed the necklace in the jumble of shiny things in the compartments.

"Yes," I lied.

"And I guess you saw her name engraved on it. Well." She sighed. "It was stupid, it was just one of those crazy impulse things, the night of the cheer dinner. Everyone was all over her, saying she led us to the state finals, you know, because she was captain and all, and it was just—I was just so tired of her getting credit for everything all the time. I mean, she partied a lot too, she was just better at covering it up. Clare . . . There's something I've never told you."

"What?" I asked carefully, keeping my voice neutral.

"Freshman year, I didn't get into Gold Key. I had some . . . trouble in middle school, and there were these seniors—there was this bitch Nell Thornton who got her friends to blackball me. Even though I was a legacy."

"I'm sorry."

"My mom had a fit. She was so angry. . . . She said she was ashamed of me. She kept talking about how it was my own fault, that she'd warned me something like that could happen. I mean, Clare, I hadn't even done anything all that bad. Not in middle school, anyway. I got caught, that was the only difference between me and lots of other people. It got all blown out of proportion, and Nell—I don't know. It all got to me, though, and I ended up . . . I had kind of a breakdown."

"It's okay," I said, putting my arm around her.

"And I got better. I really did. But then to see Amanda at that dinner that night—anyway, I knew it was a mistake right after I took the necklace. In fact I was planning to sneak it back in there the next time I was at her house. I actually had it in my purse the night she disappeared. It was the only reason I agreed to go with her that night. But then when I got over there, she didn't want to go up to her room. She was afraid her parents would wake up, so we just left, and I didn't have a chance to put it back.

"We took the cliff road because Amanda wanted to stay off Ridge. She said if someone saw us and her mom found out we weren't really down at the coffee shop, she'd be furious. And no one ever takes the cliff road at night. Anyway, she started texting Jack. I told her to stop, I told her—I was scared, you know? It's so dark there, there's no streetlights, and she was weaving all over the road."

Rachel pulled her hand back, covering her face with it. Her shoulders shook and I knew she was crying, but she made so little noise. I wanted to comfort her but I didn't know how.

"So you were in the car," I said, just to make sure. She nodded, her muffled sobs disappearing into the breeze. "But Rachel . . . you really *didn't* do anything wrong. Nobody could say . . . I mean, you asked her to stop, and she wouldn't, and there wasn't anything else you could do."

Rachel spoke through her fingers. "She was hysterical, screaming, she wanted to go down the cliff after him. I knew I couldn't let her, but I didn't know what to do. It was *me* who called her mom, Clare—I didn't know what else to do. And then I called my mom too. I told her to come as fast as she could."

The images had been building in my head since I left the Stavros house. Amanda driving away from the accident, leaving Dillon's broken body on the rocks. Both girls shivering in the cold, looking over the edge, Rachel trying to keep Amanda from following Dillon down the deadly drop.

Both mothers, driving along the deserted road to the accident site with only one thing on their minds—protecting their daughters.

The terrible conversation they must have had before they sent the girls home, Mrs. Slade following in her car while Mrs. Stavros drove to the truck stop.

"We brought Amanda home with us. Mom gave her something—I don't know, a pill she had left over from when Dad hurt his back earlier that year. It knocked her out right away. Mom gave me half of one, but I didn't fall asleep. I thought for sure she would tell Dad. But she never did. He was watching a game he had recorded, and Mom put me and Amanda in my bed, sitting in my room with us until I fell asleep. When I got up the next day, I felt all wrong from the medication, and Amanda's mom had already come for her. My mom sat me down and told me how we were never, ever going to talk about it again. That it was a terrible accident and there wasn't any point in letting it cause any more pain than it already had."

Tears leaked down her face, dripping onto her sweatshirt, and she looked at me out of the corners of her pretty blue eyes, now swollen. "It was really hard for a long time, Clare."

"I know," I said, and I meant it. I too had kept a secret, but I saw now that mine was nowhere near as heavy a burden as Rachel's. "I'm sorry."

"Me too."

"Did you . . . Did you and Amanda ever talk about it?"

Rachel blew out her breath. "We never talked again,

period. I mean, whenever I saw her at school we were all friendly like nothing had happened. She never called me or anything. The police never came close to figuring out what really happened. For the longest time everyone thought it was just an accident. And then . . . You know, the next year Amanda was gone."

"Listen, Rachel, I know you think the Grangers put that note on your windshield, but they never knew what happened to Dillon. No one does. And what you said about Mr. Granger—"

"I'm sorry, I should never have said that," Rachel said, her face darkening with shame. "I know he'd never kill his own son. But he has a horrible temper—he could definitely hurt someone if he knew they killed Dillon. I mean, he put a guy in the *hospital*. He broke a bunch of bones in his *face*."

"But Rachel, how would he ever know it was you guys?"

She sighed, looking out over the water. Wisps of hair blew around her face and she brushed them absently away.

When she spoke, her voice was barely more than a whisper.

"Because I told him."

CHAPTER TWENTY

I WAS SHOCKED INTO SILENCE. Spray from the water lapping against the pier was misting up against my face, the sun was warm on my bare arms, a mother was yelling at her children to be more careful near the edge, but I barely noticed any of it.

"Did you do that?" a gruff, angry voice said above us, snapping me out of the moment. I looked up to see a tall, thick-set man blocking the sun. He was wearing the green uniform of the local police force, and though I couldn't see his eyes behind his mirrored sunglasses, he was frowning and he looked pissed.

"What?" Rachel demanded. Instantly she transformed from the frightened, vulnerable state she'd been in seconds before to the brash, belligerent girl I knew so well. Rachel was good at covering up her true feelings with a heavy dose of attitude. "We're just sitting here. Minding our own business."

"That." The cop pointed at the water below us, where

the ice cream cup was half submerged and bobbing near the surface. The pink cloud had spread out into the water like a candy-colored oil slick. "Littering."

"Oh, that was an accident," I said quickly. "We dropped it. Not on purpose. Sorry."

"Well, how about if you *accidentally* lean down there and fish it out?" the cop said, even more sarcastically, if that were possible. Then he stood there, watching, while I got down on my stomach—my bare legs touching the pier where I knew there were bird droppings—and stretched my arm out as far as I could. But I couldn't quite get the cup.

"Here," Rachel said in her bored voice, handing me the spoon from my yogurt. That did the trick—I was able to use it to snag the cup, and I scrambled back up onto my knees to hold it out to the cop.

"*I* don't want it," he said, already turning to go. "Make sure it ends up in the trash."

When he was out of earshot, Rachel grabbed my arm and tugged. "Let's walk," she said.

Rachel headed down toward the end of the pier, which jutted far out into the ocean. It got chillier near the far end and the waves crashed up against the pilings, so walking there meant getting wet, which kept people away from the end, so we had plenty of privacy. Right now there were only two people, a couple hugging and laughing as they looked out at the sea.

"I know you're going to ask me why I haven't told the cops about Mr. Granger. But did you see what just happened?

There's your answer. The cops in Winston are losers. They can barely write traffic tickets. If I turned him in, they'd dick around and screw up the case and meanwhile I'd end up dead the minute he found out I told them."

"Rachel, what do you mean by *you* told him?"

"Well, I told *her*. Mrs. Granger. And she told him."

"When?"

"I went to the funeral. Everyone did. It was so sad. I didn't want to go but Mom said we all had to. I wore that blue dress, the one with the crossover front. I just thought about other things, you know, just trying to get through it. And I did okay.

"But then, after, when we were all leaving—I was going over to Victoria's—we walked right past the limo that was going to take Mr. and Mrs. Granger to the cemetery. The door was open and a lady was helping Mrs. Granger get into the car. I could see Mr. Granger was already inside but he was just staring out the window on the other side, and this lady, I don't know, maybe it was her sister or friend or whatever, she was trying to get Mrs. Granger to pick up her feet and get them in the car so she could close the door. But she wouldn't."

Rachel looked into my eyes, like she was searching for answers there. "It was like she had forgotten how to move. She was holding on to this other lady's arms and her face was . . . Clare, it was so weird, it was like it was sinking in, her eyes were all weird and staring and her mouth—her lipstick had all come off and she was kind of making this moaning sound with her lips pressed together. It was like her face was just going to collapse or something. Honestly, I can't remember anything after that, until later when we went over to Victoria's house and her mom was trying to get us to talk about our feelings but her dad told her just to order pizza. It was okay, later, I just pretended everything was fine. A couple of the kids had younger brothers and sisters who were in Dillon's class, and they were talking about remembering him. I stayed out of it, I sat by myself and listened.

"But I couldn't stop thinking about what Mrs. Granger had looked like. I tried to talk to my mom about it but she said the only way we were going to put it behind us was to treat it like it never happened. She said after a while it would be like it really *didn't* happen. But I couldn't stop thinking about it. Amanda wouldn't answer my texts, and at school she didn't talk to me. I couldn't sleep, I cut school a couple times . . . One day I just went over there. To the Grangers' house. I thought—I thought she had a right to know. And I also thought—I mean, it felt like I was never going to sleep again. Not unless I explained it to her. I just didn't want her wondering how Dillon had managed to go through that break in the guardrail, I kept imagining her lying awake trying to picture how it had happened. I thought . . . I know this probably sounds crazy, but I thought she might have some peace if she knew it wasn't his fault. That none of it was his fault."

She hugged herself, shivering in the cold air.

"What did she say?" I asked, afraid of the answer. "When you told her about Amanda and you, what did she say?"

"She . . ." Rachel bit her lip and stared past me, out at the ocean. "She didn't say anything for a while. She started crying. She was making these sounds like . . . like I never heard anyone make before. I started crying too, and she told me, she told me . . ." Sobs wracked Rachel's body as I put my arms around her and hugged her. She felt so insubstantial, so light. "She pushed me toward the front door and I couldn't stop crying. She said, 'You've taken everything from us. Dillon was our everything.'"

"But—Rachel. She didn't come right out and threaten Amanda, right? She didn't say, like, '*We're* going to get her' or anything like that, did she?"

Rachel pulled away from me, wiping her eyes on her sleeve.

"No, not exactly," she admitted.

"And how does she act around you now?"

"Like she always does—super nice all the time. But that doesn't mean anything. She could have told Mr. Granger, and then he went after Amanda. She might not even know he did it."

"Don't you think she'd be suspicious? If all of a sudden Amanda disappeared after she told him?"

"Maybe . . . maybe they decided together. Or maybe she just wants to be in denial about it. I don't know."

"Rachel, I still think it's a stretch. The police think it was a stranger—"

"No." Rachel shook her head. With her hair glinting gold in the sun and bringing out her blue eyes, she looked like herself again. "No. It was him. And ever since then, I've known he was watching me. Waiting."

"Is that the real reason you guys are leaving town tonight?"

Rachel nodded, her hair covering half her face. "Mom told Dad we ought to get out of town because the festival was going to be crazy. She made the hotel reservations ages ago. He has no idea what's really going on. I mean, it's like this secret she and I have in the family, and I'm not allowed to ever bring it up, even with her." Her voice quaked as she added, "I hate that, Clare. I hate having secrets in the family. It makes me feel really . . ."

I knew what she was going to say even before the wind took her final whispered word and carried it away. I knew because I'd felt it too, felt it so deep it was like it was a part of me, in my blood, lodged in my bones.

"Alone."

• • •

Rachel had to get home to finish her packing, and I was glad her parents were both home, getting ready for the trip. I didn't want her to be alone.

She seemed fine when she dropped me off. Rachel had always had an uncanny ability to switch from one mood to another. I'd always thought she was just really good at keeping her feelings pushed down and locked away. Now I knew better. She was more fragile than most people would ever know.

I felt like I had no control over my own emotions lately. Worse, I felt like something else—my gift, or else the inanimate objects that brought it out—was in charge of me rather than the other way around.

Ever since I'd touched the jacket, I'd gotten deeper and deeper into a situation that I had nothing to do with. At every step I unearthed secrets about people they would do anything to keep hidden. And I had yet to find any reason for them not to stay hidden, since nothing would ever bring Dillon or Amanda back.

Until today. If Rachel was right, she was truly in danger. She could escape for the time being, but she would never really be safe here as long as Mr. Granger's rage fueled his desire for vengeance. And how could a parent ever let go of their grief over the loss of a child? Mrs. Stavros had basically stopped living. Mr. Granger had chosen rage instead. Neither choice offered much solace, but who was I to judge?

Sitting at the kitchen table, picking at some leftover pizza I'd found in the fridge, I went back and forth. Either Amanda's death was unrelated to Dillon's, and she'd been taken by a stranger who was walking free somewhere . . . or what? Or Amanda had been killed by Mr. Granger. And maybe that had been enough to satisfy his desire for vengeance. But Winston was a small town, and Rachel was one of its stars. Everyone knew her and everyone liked her—teachers, kids from school, parents—and girls like that are far from invisible. When she marched in the homecoming parade in the fall with the cheer squad, would Mr. Granger be watching? When the local paper ran an article about the philanthropy club's beach cleanup day, would Mr. Granger read about its president? When he was at the Dell Market picking up a few things for dinner, would he see Rachel with a group of kids buying sodas?

And how long would it be until his rage boiled over and he decided he couldn't stand to see Rachel happy anymore, when his son was dead?

Maybe that was why the jacket had found me. Maybe I was being asked not just to understand what had happened, but to prevent Mr. Granger from hurting Rachel. If I could somehow help her prove what Mr. Granger had done, he would be locked up and Rachel would be safe.

An idea was forming on the edges of my mind, a plan for doing just that. I was far from ready, but as I pushed the cold pizza crust around on my plate, I couldn't seem to stop myself from wondering. Thinking.

Planning.

The jacket was safe in its hiding place in the cellar. There might be evidence on it—something to tie it to Mr. Granger. Of course, I'd touched it too, but I couldn't do anything about that now. There must have been dozens of fingerprints on it.

Scraping my plate into the trash, I washed up the dishes and then, almost like I'd been meaning to all along, I found myself standing on my porch looking out at the ocean and texting Jack.

• • •

"Are you sure this is okay?" I asked as Jack led me to a bench two doors down from the veterinary offices. He was wearing a light blue scrub shirt over his jeans, and there were some questionable stains on it. Even so, he still managed to look amazing. His hair was doing this thing where it was falling in his eyes on one side, and the more he pushed it back, the more it fell forward again.

"Yeah, I can clean cages anytime. Besides, you heard Arthur."

Jack's uncle Arthur had practically pushed us out the door, telling Jack to take as long a break as he wanted. Arthur wasn't what I expected. Yes, I could kind of tell he was sick; he was thin and he wore a skullcap over his bald head that made him look more like a rock star than anything else. He had a huge smile, and I could see glints of gold on his back teeth, like a happy pirate, what with the cap and all. Shaking my hand enthusiastically, he told me I was always welcome and made a joke about offering me something to eat but that all they had was pet treats.

It was hard not to like Arthur. I could totally see why Nana and he got along. All around the office were posters for animal causes. I even thought I saw a couple flyers for Nana's loggerhead turtle rescue group.

And Jack seemed different around him. Not more talkative, but less . . . grim. Less volatile. Calmer.

"So. What's going on, Clare?" he asked as we walked out of the office.

"I . . . need your help. With something. A . . . thing I need to do."

"You got it."

If he hadn't answered like that—instantly, no questions asked, no gotta-check-my-calendar, I might not have had the guts to tell him everything. I probably would have gotten even more tongue-tied and ended up asking a lot of dumb questions about anything else. But when I didn't answer for a minute, Jack put out his fingers, touching my cheek and turning my face so I had to look at him. He didn't smile.

"Clare—it's *me*. Tell me what you need."

I shivered, both from his touch and from the way he always looked right into my eyes, as though nothing he found there could disappoint him.

I started with what Rachel had told me and then I told him what I needed to do. People drove in and out of the office parking lot, hurrying into the dry cleaners and the phone store and the bakery. A few people came with cat carriers and dogs on leashes, but none of them paid us any attention at all, and when I was done Jack just nodded, wrapping his hand around mine.

"So." I took a deep breath, not looking at him. "I wouldn't blame you if you thought I ought to be locked up or something."

"The Grangers will be over at the festival all day. I'll pick you up around noon, okay?"

Of course I said yes. Sharing my fears with Jack, knowing that he was willing to help, even if I was wrong, even if I was crazy, made it better already. I walked back into the clinic with him—he'd bought his uncle a cookie, despite the fact that Arthur probably wouldn't eat it—and said good-bye. I promised Arthur I would come back again soon, give my love to my grandmother, and let him know the minute I talked my mom into a pet so he could discuss her options with her.

As I left, I felt a kind of hope that I wasn't sure was warranted. After all, we were about to do something really risky—maybe even stupid. And yet, when I biked away from the shopping center, I felt more sure than I had in a long time.

CHAPTER TWENTY-ONE

"What's this?" I asked as I got into Jack's truck the next day. I'd promised my mom I'd meet her at the festival in the afternoon and we could walk around together. No matter what we found, this expedition wasn't going to take that long.

On the seat was a brown bag, the top rolled over like a lunch sack, but when I picked it up it was heavy and made a clanking sound.

Jack shot me a look. "Breaking and entering one-oh-one. I looked it up on the Internet."

"Oh, no . . ." I opened the bag and looked in: a thin strip of metal, a screwdriver, a file, some wire. "Are you sure—I mean, with, you know—"

"My police record?" Jack asked. "Yeah. Wouldn't look good. So, let's not get caught, okay?"

He sounded calm; only the slightest edge to his voice gave any hint that he had any concerns about what we were going to do. I felt guilty already, asking him to come with me, but I hadn't thought about what would happen if we got caught. I guess I was thinking I would just make up some story on the spot. Maybe I'd be believable, maybe I wouldn't, but the odds were that as a good kid who'd never been in any kind of trouble before, I'd be able to fake my way out of it.

But Jack? Not so much. He'd been accused of things a lot worse than sneaking into a stranger's house, and I would guess that the detective he'd told me about, the one who seemed so disappointed not to be able to pin Amanda's disappearance on him, would be more than happy to have something else to focus on.

"Look, Jack—maybe I should do this alone. I mean, it's not all that complicated. I'll just make sure no one's home and then I'll only need about a half hour. You could wait for me a few blocks away."

"No." Jack was already shaking his head before I finished speaking. "No way I'm letting you go in there alone."

"But if I make sure no one's home, nothing can happen," I pointed out, reasonably.

Jack's stormy glare told me otherwise. "No. I'm coming with you or I'm turning around and taking you home."

I opened my mouth to respond, then closed it again. Jack's determination made me feel safe.

He parked on a street parallel to the Grangers', in front of a house that was under construction. I was new to the whole wrong-side-of-the-law thing, and as Jack and I walked, I tried to channel my nervousness into acting normal. When I touched his hand he wrapped it around mine.

"Just walk around the side like we belong here," he said. "We could be watering her plants or taking care of her cat."

We didn't see anyone in the streets. Everyone was probably down at the festival, along with the hundreds of out-of-towners who'd come for the day. I followed Jack down a walkway on the side of the tidy ranch house, toward a wooden gate, and Jack dug into his pocket and pulled out some plastic gloves.

"Put these on," he said. "It's just in case, worst-case scenario, the Grangers think they've had a break-in—the cops won't find our prints."

"Oh, Jack, do you really—"

"I'm in the system," he said quietly. "You've never been printed, but I have. If they get a match—"

I slipped on the gloves. On the other side of the gate was a walkway leading to a neatly mowed backyard edged in empty flower beds. Everything was tidy, but there were no signs that anyone had been enjoying the patio. The furniture was covered and the grill looked untouched.

"Sliding glass door," Jack said, scanning the back of the house, "and that window's open. We can get in that way. But before we try . . ."

I followed him around the other side to where a door led into the garage. Jack tried the knob; it opened easily.

"Yeah," he said softly. "And what do you want to bet . . ."

The garage was lined with exercise equipment and gardening tools, golf clubs and sports gear, all of it neatly stored but dusty from lack of use. Jack tried the door to the house.

Open.

Inside he shut the door behind us, very carefully. The kitchen was dim, the blinds over the sink lowered, blocking out natural light. An African violet sat on the windowsill, along with bottles of prescription medication and a china figurine of a boy in a baseball uniform taking a swing. A pot of cooking utensils shared counter space with a set of canisters and an empty drying rack: no evidence of a recent meal. A newspaper lay unopened on the kitchen table.

The house, as carefully maintained as it was, felt sad. I knew I was probably projecting my own feelings, but as I looked around the sparse living room beyond the kitchen, the drapes shut tight so that only a few bars of sun slanted across the sofas and the entertainment center, I got the feeling that the people who lived here weren't really living anymore. That they were just marking time, going to work and coming home and getting up to try to get through another day. It wasn't like Mrs. Stavros's home, where everything would have disintegrated even more if she didn't have friends or family checking in on her, where grief and longing were as dense as perfume in the air. Here, it seemed as though Mr. and Mrs. Granger were just going through the motions.

And then I saw the pictures.

I'd missed them at first because it was so dark in the house, but as my eyes adjusted to the dimness I saw that every frame on the wall, the shelves, the coffee tables, the entertainment center—every one of them held photos of a boy, from infancy to age ten. Dillon. There had to be a couple dozen of them, some of them studio shots in nice frames, many more baseball portraits and team photos. Candid shots covered the refrigerator and were tucked into the corners of cabinets.

And there—in plain black frames lining the hallway—were the newspaper articles. "Local Boy Lost to Cliffs Accident." "Seacliff Road's Deadly Twist Takes Another." "Winston Mourns One Lost Too Soon."

Two of the three articles featured the same picture—Dillon, laughing, in his baseball uniform—and the third showed Mr. and Mrs. Granger lighting a candle at a remembrance service. Mrs. Granger looked surprisingly young and pretty, despite the terrible grief in her eyes. She had attractive features, thick brown hair down past her shoulders, and her husband—his face completely blank, as though he were feeling nothing at all—stood slightly to the side.

"It's like a tomb in here," Jack said softly, coming up behind me.

"Let's find their room." I led Jack down the hall past a formal living room, where the only decorations were pictures of Dillon and a signed baseball in an acrylic display case, arranged around a crystal candy dish. We passed a bathroom that smelled like bleach, and a bedroom I assumed was meant for guests, with its bare, plain furniture and bed made up with extra pillows and a folded throw.

Jack opened a door that had been left closed and I knew immediately that it was Dillon's room. Everything was as it must have been the day he died—there were baseball cleats on the floor along with a wadded pair of slider pants. Textbooks and papers littered his desk. The bed had been made, a stuffed lion with a loopy yarn mane sitting on top of the pillow.

If the rest of the house was sad, this room was down-right haunting. It was like the shadow of Dillon was still here in every corner, and of course that must have been why his parents kept the room like this. I wondered if Mrs. Granger came in here and just stood in the middle of the room, not touching anything, remembering the many times she had tucked him in at night, toweled him off from a bath, helped him pick up his toys, read him a book. I wondered if the room would still be like this next month, next year.

I turned away. "I'll be down the hall," I said.

"Okay. I'm going to look around in here."

The Grangers' master bedroom was as bland as the rest of the house, with beige carpet and drapes and bed linens. A man's cargo shorts and polo shirt were draped over an armchair, and I guessed that Mr. Granger changed into ca-sual clothes when he came home from work, leaving them on the chair when he went to bed. I thought of how angry he always seemed, and about the man he put in the hospi-tal, and wondered if he took his anger out on Mrs. Granger too, maybe even here in this soulless room.

There were so many emotions in my head already, and I knew that I had to clear my mind if I was going to be able to do what I came here for. Enough procrastinating. I went to the closet—it was a large walk-in space separated down the middle into his and hers—and stripped off my gloves, stuffing them into my pocket, since I could only read clothes when I touched them with my bare skin. I started with the golf shirts in a neat row on the top, reaching for a gray one.

Holding the fabric lightly between my fingertips, I closed my eyes. I concentrated on opening myself to Mr. Granger's memories, but there was nothing. I moved slowly down the closet bar through the rest of his shirts, gently touching them and letting them fall back in place, but they were nothing but ordinary cotton and synthetic fabric.

I resented being here, resented the vision that had seized me when I touched the denim jacket, resented its insistence that I find out what happened. It wasn't a job I had asked for. It wasn't one I was well qualified for. I had never even met Amanda—but now I felt like I was connected to her, like she had chosen me.

At some point I had gone through all the shirts and moved on to the pants and shorts. None of this was what I needed. There were no visions at all. Whatever Mr. Granger had worn when he punched the dad from the other team, or threatened the referees and got himself ejected from games, he no longer owned. And if he'd gotten rid of all the clothes Amanda had worn, why would he keep what he was wearing? If he had any sense at all he would have disposed of those first, in case there was some sort of evidence on them. I didn't know anything about forensics besides what I saw on TV, but they were always finding a fiber or a hair or something and solving crimes with them. Odds were that Mr. Granger was smart enough to throw the clothes away.

"Anything?" It was Jack, standing in the entry to the closet.

"No . . . not yet. Listen, I'm going to see if he's got anything in the guest bedroom closet. Can you go through the dresser drawers in here and see if there are any T-shirts, I don't know, maybe something that looks a little older?"

Jack put his hand on my shoulder as I passed, turning me toward him; I looked into his eyes and knew he was worried about me.

"Are you doing all right?" he asked softly.

I forced a smile. "Yes, fine. There's nothing here. It's just clothes."

Jack nodded and let me go. I hadn't told him the entire truth—that even without the visions, the experience of being in the Grangers' home was difficult. Even if I was imagining the emotions that seemed to weigh down the sad rooms, my imagination was powerful and my feelings real.

In the hall I had a new thought—*What about the coat closet?* The weather along the coast could be chilly even in the middle of summer. Especially at night. The locals rarely went anywhere without a windbreaker or jacket, and everyone loved to make fun of the tourists shivering outside the Frosty Top on cool summer nights, eating their ice cream with goose bumps covering their arms.

The coat closet was jammed, and I reached for the hangers, meaning to push all the garments to one side so I could go through them one by one. But as my fingers brushed against the different fabrics, I was suddenly hit by a ferocious, body-slamming jolt.

It was like with Amanda's jacket, except . . . sharper, somehow, and bitter. As my hand roved back, settling on the coat that had provoked me, it was bitterness that filled my mind, my gut, my senses. It was the taste in my mouth, like poison, like . . . vengeance.

And I knew I'd found the one when my fingers brushed against slick, vinyl-coated fabric that flamed with energy. Carefully I lifted the hanger from the rack, not touching the fabric, my heart pounding. It was a knee-length rain-coat, constructed from a cotton or polyester blend that had been coated to make it waterproof. It was red, with a stitched-on belt and big silver-tone buttons, and it had a bit of flare below the waist. A nice coat, one that would have cost more because of the details but that was time-less, the sort of thing my mom would buy if it came in a boring gray.

I took a deep breath and grabbed two fistfuls of red fabric.

Rage. My head split with it, my face burned with it; my fingers were clutched so tight my knuckles hurt. I was a thing of fury, my senses drowning with an anger that filled every cell of my being.

I could barely breathe, and I tried to let go of the fabric for a moment so I could catch my breath, collect myself before trying again. Instead, the coat seemed to clutch me tighter . . . and the vision tumbled into my mind.

Hair. Bright, glossy, reflecting . . . Or it was the moon? Amanda's hair in the moonlight, tangled but still beautiful, dragging on the ground. I was dragging her. And oh, God, she

*was heavy, but it wouldn't be much longer, would it? Just a
little farther. Just a little farther . . . rough, uneven earth. No
path, just the dirt under my shoes. White shoes. Keds, with laces
neatly tied. Amanda's face . . . Dear God, what had happened to
her face? One half looked like her picture, but the other half
looked like—*

Blood on my jeans. Blood on my Keds.

Blood under my fingernails.

*Her face bloody, her cheekbone broken, I can see the bone pro-
truding. Her mouth torn. Rage, I want to feel it again, crashing
heavy down on that pretty face, that face that didn't look where
she was going, that face that killed my baby.*

*Heaving. Breathing hard. Dragging. But there. There, fi-
nally, we are at the edge. The cinderblocks are there. Four of
them . . . so heavy, so heavy, carrying them one by one, the edges
ground into my chest, the soft skin on the underside of my wrists.
My blood mixing with hers. Sweat is pouring down my forehead but the air is cold on my face.*

*The car up on the dirt tracks. The weeds flattened, can't help
that. The edge of the pond lapping against the crusted dirt, like
it took bites out of the shore. Pretty at night, silvery, shiny, but
during the day it's the dirt brown of every farm pond. Flat and
still. No one would want to wade in this pond. No one would
swim here. The skiff upside down on the dirt hasn't been used in
many months, maybe years. I'll put it back where I found it. A
few days of dust blowing will leave a coat of grit on its surface,
no one will know about its journey tonight.*

*There. Drop her arms. They make a smacking sound on the
plastic tarp I've used to drag her, the one that kept the blood out*

of my car. Her mouth is open. I use my foot to push her jaw shut, but not too hard. Into the skiff, dragging it into the water. Just a little, don't want her getting any ideas, floating away without me. There's the rope. Bristly. It hurts my scratched-up wrists but that's okay, this will just take . . . Tying, tying, pulling tight, the skiff rocks when I drop the blocks in.

Rest? No, I can't. I wipe my forehead on my coat sleeve, gulping air. Push off. One oar . . . Should there be two? Is it lost in the bottom of the pond, well, soon it will have company. How far out: at first I think the middle of the pond but I am very tired now, just a little farther . . . I put the oar on the floor of the skiff as I pick up one of the blocks and dump it in the water. Her arm makes a cracking sound. I get the second block in and she is perched on the edge of the skiff now as though she is hugging it, holding on, and for a minute it's like she doesn't want to go and I feel sad for her. But then I think about what she did to my baby, my angel, and the other blocks seem to weigh a lot less. Splash. Splash. Gone.

CHAPTER TWENTY-TWO

THE FABRIC FELL FROM MY CLUTCHED fists, my fingers aching as I flexed them open. Had I blacked out? I was breathing hard, and the sweat on my face was real. I was leaning against the coat closet's doorjamb and it was cutting into the skin of my shoulder. The red sleeve had fallen back against the coat, which had slipped partway off the hanger. I did not want to touch it again. I did not want to touch it *ever* again. I heard a sound and realized it was me saying something like "Oh God oh God," and I swallowed, backing up, and ran right into something.

Some*one*. They stumbled from the impact and I thought, *Please please be Jack,* but I somehow knew it wasn't. As she wrapped her arm around my neck I wondered how long she'd been watching me.

"I told her to be careful," Mrs. Granger hissed against my ear. "I told her I'd be watching her."

Her breath smelled like coffee and cinnamon gum, and she was surprisingly strong, or maybe it just seemed that way because the vision had left me weak and shaky. This was Amanda's killer, I knew it for certain now, and even though part of me knew that I was in terrible, terrible trouble, there was another small part that was at peace for the first time since I had opened the box and touched the denim jacket.

But I hadn't been meant simply to find out the truth: I needed to stop Amanda's killer from hurting Rachel. I twisted as hard as I could, and was rewarded with a sharp pain in my side.

"Don't you dare," Mrs. Granger said, and I saw the knife in her hand. "I'm not going to kill you on my nice carpet. Isn't this convenient, me coming home just now, today of all days? Do you want to know where I killed Amanda? Right there, in my kitchen. I was ready for her. She didn't even notice. I called her and told her I wanted to talk to her, and that evil girl was so hungry for forgiveness she was here practically before I hung up the phone."

"Please," I managed, my teeth chattering with fear. It was incredibly eerie to hear the hateful words coming from the woman who'd been so kind to me when she stood on my front porch, who'd greeted us so warmly at her son's memorial.

Where is Jack? Shouldn't he be finished in the other room by now?

Mrs. Granger pulled her arm tighter against my neck and I started to choke. Ordinarily I would have been a match for her, but I was shaking too hard, my arms and legs rubbery and twitching with the prickly sensation I some-times felt after a vision.

"My husband had gone to the store. We were out of Tylenol," she murmured almost dreamily. "He started get-ting the headaches, you see, after we lost Dillon. I told him if I felt up to it I might go see my sister, and not to worry if I was gone when he got back. I'd always wondered what I would do if I came face to face with Amanda, and here she was, *she* came to *me*. She was standing right over there. And do you want to know something, Clare? I watch Rachel. I watch you girls. I came by your little stand the other week. You didn't even recognize me. I had on sunglasses and a hat." She chuckled, as though proud of herself. "You have talent. I'll give you that. And Rachel . . . Such a pretty girl, you can't even tell she's rotten on the inside. Evil."

"She's not . . . We're not . . ." I was trying to scream, to summon Jack from wherever he'd gone, but Mrs. Granger had cut off almost all my air and I could barely manage a whisper. *She's not evil,* I wanted to say. Neither was Amanda. She had just made a horrible mistake.

I was starting to black out, and it was nothing like the visions: it was terrifying. I was going to die here in the kitchen. I kicked as hard as I could but my feet were just shuffling on the floor.

Maybe this time Rachel would be brave enough to go to the police with what she knew, but she had guessed wrong. She'd give them the wrong name. How could we ever have imagined it was Mrs. Granger, with her pink lipstick and her kind smile and her pearls? Besides, without knowing where Amanda's body was, they would never be able to convict Mrs. Granger.

"I'll have to kill her too," Mrs. Granger said, sounding more matter-of-fact than unhappy about it. "All three of you. But that ought to wrap things up. You haven't told anyone else, have you? No? Well, it will all be over soon. You know, Dusty keeps saying we need to start to move on. Can you believe that? I mean, he's Dillon's *father*, how he can—"

Mrs. Granger suddenly pushed me into the closet, sending me toppling into the clothes as I put out my hands too late to break my fall. I heard her howl with anger, and then came another voice:

"Stay there, Clare!"

It was Jack, and I was so relieved that I ignored him and crawled out on my hands and knees.

He was much stronger than Mrs. Granger, and he had her around the waist, but she was kicking at his feet and stabbing wildly with the knife as he tried to grab her arm. I saw with horror that she'd already managed to cut him— the sleeve of his T-shirt was stained with blood.

She was aiming for his neck, fighting as hard as she could, making sounds like an angry cornered dog. With the last of my strength I reached for the fabric of her pants, grabbing as much in my hand as I could, and pulled. She screamed, tripping backward, and I heard the clatter of the knife on the floor right before she landed on me, knocking the wind out of me.

Jack dragged her away and the fabric slipped out of my fingers, but not before I caught a glimpse of the bleak, poisoned place that Mrs. Granger's mind had become.

. . .

Jack never took his gloves off, so the only fingerprints we had to wipe away were the ones on the closet door. It didn't take too long—my strength came back quickly once I got away from the coat and Mrs. Granger.

I watched Jack tie her up to a kitchen chair, wondering if the rope he found in the garage was the same rope she'd used to tie the weights to Amanda before she tipped her into the livestock pond. Jack had taped her mouth, taking care not to hurt her, not until I'd asked her a couple of questions. She strained against the rope and tried to scream, so Jack clapped his hand over her mouth and nose until she stopped struggling and got more cooperative.

She told us Amanda had been wearing the jacket when she dragged her across the field to the farm pond. It had come off her body along the way, and when Mrs. Granger discovered it lying on the ground on her way back to her car, she knew she had to get rid of it. Even as filthy and torn as the jacket had become, it was still a loose thread.

She'd dumped the jacket at the landfill on the way home.

As I sat shivering, thinking about the jacket's strange path from Amanda to me, I didn't miss the confidence with which Jack handled Mrs. Granger. I wondered if it came from working in the clinic. In a way, Mrs. Granger had something in common with the other dangerous animals they occasionally saw, the ones bred for fighting or ruined by abuse. Mrs. Granger had been ruined, too, but she couldn't just be put down like a rabid coyote or a pit bull who'd attacked a child.

"Here's what's going to happen now," Jack said calmly when she was finally secured to the chair, silent and still. "We're going to make a call tonight. They'll be searching all the farm ponds in the county by tomorrow. I don't think you'll have to wait too long."

Mrs. Granger made muffled, angry sounds from her chair, twisting her body as much as the rope would allow.

"I wouldn't tell them about us if I were you," I said, my voice scratchy from my throat being squeezed so hard. "Not about Rachel, either. I mean, you could, but then we're going to have to tell them that you invited me and Rachel here because you planned to kill us. I'll tell them how I brought Jack instead, and you tried to hurt us and we barely managed to get away . . . how we were terrified to say anything. I'll be convincing, believe me."

For a moment I felt genuine pity for the poor shell of a mother in the chair. I didn't doubt that the real Mrs. Granger had been a very different person, and I was terribly sorry that she was gone, along with her child.

But I had my own future to think about. Mine, and Jack's, and Rachel's. "But if they thought you were going to kill us, too, they might not feel so sorry for you. And don't forget, we still have the jacket. Are you willing to gamble that you left no trace of yourself on it?"

"Wait for your husband," Jack said. He'd gotten Mrs. Granger's cell phone out of her purse and found Mr. Granger's mobile number at the top of the favorites list. He'd written a text saying to come home right away, that there had been an emergency. All that was left was to hit "Send."

"Ask for his forgiveness. Maybe he'll stand by you. I guess you could try running . . . if he was even willing to let you. . . . But you wouldn't have much of a head start."

Mrs. Granger sagged against the chair, the rope cutting into her shoulders. The fight suddenly appeared to go out of her. I had to admit it was a pretty good plan—far from foolproof, but the best we could do.

Jack looked questioningly at me, his thumb poised over the "Send" button.

"Ready?"

CHAPTER TWENTY-THREE

A WEEK BEFORE SCHOOL STARTED, Mom and I threw a dinner party.

Mom had walked up Grover Hill earlier in the week with a bottle of sparkling wine and a basket of freshly baked empanadas—and hadn't come home until after midnight, her eyes puffy and red but her face lit with a hopeful smile. I had a feeling Nana's visits were going to be more frequent from now on.

In fact, I had been getting the china out of the sideboard on Sunday morning when Mom came into the dining room wearing a shirt she'd never worn before, her hair in a ponytail. "No, no, honey, let's try something else tonight. I was going through some things. . . ."

All day long Mom pulled boxes from storage, unearthing all kinds of keepsakes and heirlooms I'd never seen before. Some had even been given to her by Dad's mom before she died, and when I asked Mom if she wanted to send them to Dad out in Sacramento, she frowned for a moment and then laughed.

"You know, I doubt the cheap bastard would miss any of this—let's just not tell him."

She had never, ever said a negative word about my dad before, but as I watched her take out the colorful embroidered napkins his mom had brought over from Czechoslovakia, the shell-handled teaspoons, the red glass goblets—all the while singing along with a Rolling Stones CD I'd had no idea she owned—I realized there was a lot more to my mom than I knew.

The shirt she was wearing, by the way, was one I'd made for her a couple of years earlier. It had started life as a simple linen blouse, but I'd belled the sleeves and added vertical rows of silk ribbon up the placket. At the time she'd said it had a sort of gypsy charm, but I'd never seen her wear it until today. Now she hummed and sashayed around in it like it was her favorite thing ever.

Jack would be over soon to help before the rest of the guests—Nana and her new boyfriend, Rachel, and Jack's uncle Arthur—arrived. When everything seemed to be under control, I went to my room to wrap the little gift I'd found to cheer Rachel up.

I'd been teaching her simple cross-stitch, and I'd found a set of vintage pillowcases stamped with a retro sunflower design at a garage sale the week before. They were perfect, especially after I added some embroidery floss that I had in my thread box. We'd recently spent a few nights watching old movies, talking and stitching, and Rachel needed a new project.

I knew she'd be fine eventually, but after Amanda's body was found in a livestock pond four miles southeast of town, Rachel kind of lost it, and I'd been spending a lot of time with her. It was hard to keep everything I knew to myself, but I'd decided not to tell her about my gift for now. As far as Rachel knew, Mrs. Granger had had a fit of conscience, and her husband had driven her to the police station so she could confess to killing Amanda after Amanda admitted hitting Dillon with her car. Mrs. Granger never mentioned Rachel at all, and Rachel was finally starting to believe that she was now safe, especially since Mrs. Granger was awaiting sentencing in the county jail.

It was all anyone talked about. Mrs. Stavros buried her daughter on an overcast day, rain threatening to pour from rolling purple clouds, after a service attended by enough people to overflow the church yet again. After that, she wasn't seen in town, and she was rumored to be staying with her sister. My guess was that neither she nor her husband would ever return to Winston, that in time it would be like they had never lived there at all.

I went with Rachel to visit Amanda's grave one day, and she left Amanda's necklace on the smooth marble headstone.

My mom had gone out to lunch with Mrs. Slade a week after the funeral, but she told me afterward that they still didn't have much in common. Maybe it was a friendship that wasn't meant to be. But Mom had better luck with a few other people, friends from her long-ago tennis team and concert band, and before long she was going out a couple of times a week for a movie or a glass of wine.

I didn't tell her or Nana what had really happened. I decided it was best if they thought the same thing everyone else did, that Mrs. Granger had simply turned herself in. I thought that if no one knew, then things could simply stay the same. But they didn't. Maybe I was the one who changed first—after I'd learned and survived, none of the small things that used to drive me crazy seemed to matter. And Mom changed too. She must have been ready for a reconciliation with Nana, after I forced her to come to an understanding about our gift. Whatever the cause, she seemed happier and more energetic than she had in a long time.

And she had been cooking nonstop.

Every day she came home from work at a reasonable hour, loaded down with groceries and produce from the farmers' market. Soon the house would be fragrant with whatever was simmering on the stove or baking in the oven or cooling on the counter. There was always more than we could eat, and we got into a habit of going for walks after dinner, taking plates of food to the neighbors, the guys down at the fire station, and, on one occasion, the very surprised Garza brothers, the dishwashers at the Shuckster, who seemed delighted to be the recipient of Mom's zucchini-chèvre lasagna.

My Blake friends were coming down in a few days for an end-of-summer celebration before we all went back to school, and Mom had promised to help me cook and get the house ready. It would be crowded, and I was nervous about my old friends meeting my new ones, but mostly I was excited. I'd told Jack and Rachel all about Lincoln and Maura and Caleb, and I couldn't wait for them all to meet.

For tonight's party we were doing a taco bar. Mom had been smoking a pork roast all day, and its heavenly smell wafted in through our open windows. The corn was shucked and ready to grill, the salsa sitting on the counter in a pottery bowl so the flavors could blend. I had taken the flourless chocolate torte out of the oven earlier in the day and Mom had piped ganache on top once it cooled. She'd offered to let me try, but I knew she'd do a perfect job.

And I kind of wanted her to shine.

I heard Jack's knock at the front door and called for him to come on in. He was fresh from a shower, wearing a T-shirt I hadn't seen before, his damp black hair falling in his eyes. While someone else might have picked out something special for the occasion, Jack's shirt looked like it had been at the bottom of his dresser drawer since the last time he ran out of clean laundry—creased and gray and threadbare, with "Boise State" in faded script. I wondered if it had been his dad's—for sure, there was a story there. Maybe someday he'd tell me.

Jack wrapped his arms around me and almost lifted me off the floor with the force of his hug. He had greeted me like this ever since that day, when we'd left the Grangers' and driven up to the overlook, where we spent the afternoon watching the sailboats on the ocean. He'd promised to destroy the jacket for me so I would never have to see or touch it again. And I'd cried as Jack held me on the bench seat of his old truck.

I liked that he was protective of me. But I felt strong.

"Nice outfit," Jack said, raising an eyebrow.

"Thanks." I smiled, twirling for him, the skirt of my vintage sundress swirling around my legs. It was from the fifties, and there had been a few moth holes on the bodice, but I'd appliquéd several large poppies in orange and red over the damaged areas, adding rows of orange rickrack to the skirt. Josie's button hung from a silver chain around my neck. I'd dyed the ends of my hair a bright reddish-magenta the week before and I was wearing a white vinyl headband that looked either punk or retro, I couldn't decide which.

Nana was next to arrive. She was wearing a tank top that revealed a lot more of her saggy freckled cleavage than most old ladies would probably be comfortable showing. But since I was the person who'd stitched the rainbow paillettes along the neckline, I could hardly criticize. She had on one of her long flowing skirts and there were bits of leaves and grass stuck to the bottom, so I knew she hadn't been able to resist doing a little gardening on the way out of the house.

She handed Mom a big bunch of camellias tied with red and green ribbon that looked suspiciously Christmasy. "Here, Susie," she said hesitantly, her voice wobbling.

"Oh, for heaven's sake," my mom said, setting the flowers on the counter and hugging her.

I turned away to give them some privacy, smiling to

myself. The other guests were due any minute. Jack was out at the grill, so I joined him there while Mom showed Nana the table settings, the mismatched collection of dishes and silver and glassware.

Smoke billowed around us as Jack poked at the delicious-smelling slab of charred meat.

"Your mom did this?" he said. "Scary."

"What do you mean?"

"The women in your family are not to be messed with. There must be twenty pounds of pig here. Did she kill it with her bare hands too?"

I laughed. I loved that Jack thought my mom and grandmother and I were badasses, a conclusion he'd reached when I'd taken him to meet Nana and we'd found her on the roof, fixing a shingle with a hammer and a mouthful of nails.

Jack and I went to sit on the front porch to wait for the other guests. Out over the water, the sun was starting to splinter into bands of orange and pink and gold. It was going to be a beautiful sunset. Jack put his arm around my shoulders and I leaned in, breathing in his laundry and soap scent. No animal-cage smells today, that was for sure.

I knew things would change soon. New school, new friends, new classes, all kinds of challenges and distractions. I was a little nervous—okay, I was a lot nervous—but I knew I would be all right.

"We sold the last of my designs yesterday," I told him. "NewToYou is closed until next summer."

"You going to miss it?"

"Well, I think I'm going to be pretty busy with school, so any extra time I have I'm just going to work on my own stuff."

"But you still want to be a designer, right?"

"Yeah, I just thought I might . . ." I could feel myself blushing. "Uh, Mom said she'd take me up to San Jose next weekend. There's a store there, they import fabric from all over the world. Yard goods, but they have bolt ends at great discounts."

"So, you're going to keep making clothes?"

"Yes. No more hand-me-downs at the moment."

I didn't consider my gift a bad thing. I didn't feel cursed, and I was sure the day would come when I was ready to explore the visions again. But for now, I had a few designs in mind that I wanted to try making from scratch, creating the patterns and cutting out the pieces, tailoring them to my exact measurements. They'd be mine . . . truly mine, originals that no one else in the world would own. The thought filled me with pride.

"So, do they have, like, fancy fabric? At that store?"

"Um, fancy?"

"You know. Silky stuff. Like for dresses. Like . . . maybe for the homecoming dance."

"There's a homecoming dance?" I asked innocently. But I already knew the answer. Rachel had told me all about it. According to her it was kind of lame, but she was still planning to go, with Ky, if Ky was still in the picture by then.

Otherwise, she was kind of interested in Miles Baldridge, who had just gotten back from spending the summer on the East Coast with his cousins.

"Yes. There is. And you're going with me."

Oh. I felt my smile getting bigger. Yes . . . I could come up with something good. Something spectacular, even.

Inside, I heard my mother's and grandmother's voices joined in laughter. A gentle wind had picked up, and far down the hill, waves broke in white swells along the shore. Soon it would be chilly enough to get a sweater, but for now I was happy right here where I was meant to be, with a boy I was starting to fall for. My skin touched the soft, much-washed cotton of his shirt, but I sensed no emotions but my own happiness and heard no thoughts except my own.

About the Author

Sophie Littlefield is the Edgar Award–nominated author of mysteries, thrillers, and horror fiction for adults. She lives with her family in Northern California. Visit her online at sophielittlefield.com.